Margaret Wilmer

The wrecker's grandchild

Margaret Wilmer

The wrecker's grandchild

ISBN/EAN: 9783337214654

Printed in Europe, USA, Canada, Australia, Japan

Cover: Foto ©Andreas Hilbeck / pixelio.de

More available books at **www.hansebooks.com**

THE

WRECKER'S GRANDCHILD.

By MARGARET E. WILMER.

NEW YORK:

BOARD OF PUBLICATION, R. C. A.,

34 Vesey Street.

1871.

PREFACE.

THE following narrative is designed to teach a two-fold lesson:—First, it illustrates the fact that, without a living and developed Christianity, a person may possess cultivation of intellect, polish of manners, and every other pleasing and desirable attainment, and yet utterly fail in securing true peace of mind and happiness. His life may be as useless to his fellow-beings as it is unsatisfactory to himself. He will have no power to exert over others any real or personal influence for good. At the same time, it shows that the humblest and most ignorant in worldly things, if but possessed of a true faith in Christ, may be endowed with a heavenly wisdom, and a power from on high, which shall make them "mighty in word and deed." In the second place, it serves to show the importance of the *Sunday School*, as an agent for the diffusion of Christianity and civilization among the rudest, and a means not only of enlisting the children upon the side of gospel truth, but also of teaching, through those children, the hearts of grown people who often resist the efforts made in other ways to convince them of the perilous state of their souls, and to win them over to Christ.

CONTENTS.

———•+•———

CONTENTS.

———→·←———

(5)

THE
WRECKER'S GRAND-CHILD.

CHAPTER I.

THE SHIPWRECK.

DAYBREAK, upon the coast of Florida, showed a two-masted vessel, or "schooner," driven before a heavy gale, and tossed upon the waves of a boisterous sea. The only persons on board of this vessel were its owner, Richard Von Ulden, his son, his little grand-daughter, her mulatto nurse, and a boy who did the roughest of the work. Marianna, the little girl, was but three years old. Several months before, she had the sad misfortune to lose her moth-

er, and shed tears over a great, and never-to-
be - forgotten sorrow. Her grand - father,
Richard Von Ulden, was one whose whole
history would add much to the interest
of this narrative, if we could spare the
space for it. From childhood, it had been
his principal aim, to take every possible advantage of his fellow-beings, and to gain for
himself all that he could, even if others had
to suffer. When a boy, his greatest delight
was in winning marbles, or in taking pen-
nies and sweetmeats from other children, if
they happened to be younger and weaker
than himself;—while, towards those who
were as strong as he was, he employed
trickery and cheating to gain from them
what he coveted. He grew up to be a selfish, unprincipled man. He tried a variety
of speculations, was successful, and made a
great deal of money, but he forfeited the

good opinion and confidence of all who knew him. At length, in consequence of breaking the laws of the United States, a very fine vessel, which he owned, was taken from him, and sold. This was a heavy loss, for which no one pitied him; and this additional vexation made him so angry that he resolved to leave his country and go to live in Cuba. He requested his son, Marianna's father, to accompany him, and the young man consented. It must not be supposed however from this circumstance, that young Von Ulden was like his father, in character or purpose. He was a steady, industrious, upright man. Instead of being ruined by his father's example, he had the good sense to learn from it that oft-repeated, yet oft-forgotten lesson, that there is no policy so truly shrewd and wise, and so much to one's advantage as that of *honesty*.

The Von Uldens were soon upon their way to Cuba, in a vessel belonging to the old man, who, because he had once been a sea captain, insisted that he was able to serve as pilot, during the voyage. Foolish, obstinate man! In more important matters, this had been his great mistake. He had rejected Jesus, the heavenly Pilot, who could have guided him with unerring safety, and had determined to steer his own course through life.

There he stood, grasping the helm, and looking, with desperate obstinacy, straight ahead, while his vessel staggered and shook before the buffetings of the storm. His head was uncovered, his bushy, gray hair and beard were dishevelled by the gale;—his lips firmly compressed, and his fiery, blood-shot eyes almost hidden by their over-hanging brows.

Young Von Ulden, and John, the boy, did all they could in managing the vessel, and their pale, anxious faces showed that they knew the greatness of the impending danger. Little Marianna with her nurse was below, in the cabin, and the thoughts of her father dwelt almost entirely upon his helpless child.

Presently, a heavy sea dashed over the vessel, and swept young Von Ulden and John from the deck into the ocean! Marianna's father uttered one cry to his Maker, and then, with the poor, friendless lad who shared his fate, disappeared forever, amidst the roaring waves.

A groan burst from the old man's lips, and his hands, relaxing their hold of the helm, fell helpless by his sides.

At this moment, a sunken rock pierced the vessel's hull, and the water, rushing into the cabin, compelled the colored woman, Naomi, to hasten upon deck, with little Marianna

"Oh, Mr. Von Ulden, the vessel has struck!" exclaimed Naomi, "but where is Master George? Where is Johnny?"

"Ask that sea!" shouted the old man, turning his fierce and haggard countenance upon her, and pointing, with quivering finger, to the billows amidst which his son and the boy had disappeared.

Overcome with horror and grief, Naomi threw herself upon the deck, where, indeed, it would have been difficult to stand upright, on account of the rocking and plunging of the vessel. Von Ulden took no notice of her emotion, but fixed his eyes upon little Marianna. She was now the only creature upon earth whose safety he cared for, or whom he could expect to cherish any affection for him.

At one time, while with her nurse, below, in the cabin, she was very much frightened by the violence of the storm, the tossing of the vessel and the agitation which she noticed in all the persons on board. Nestling close to Naomi, and looking up in her face, she said, "My papa can save us;—can't he?"

"My dear child," answered Naomi, as she pressed her to her bosom, "your papa will do all he can; but, if we are saved, it will not be by him."

"Then it will be Gran'papa that will take us all on shore," questioned Marianna.

"The only one that can bring us safely on shore," answered Naomi, "is our Father in Heaven, whom you pray to every night and

2

morning. If we want to be safe,—now, or any other time,—we must *look to God.*"

These words were spoken very earnestly, and they made a deep impression on the infant mind of Marianna, for she knew that her good nurse never deceived her. Thenceforth, she was quiet, and, taking Naomi's advice to "look to God," in the literal sense, she kept her eyes raised towards Heaven, where she knew that her Divine Father dwelt.

When the waves burst into the cabin, and Naomi with her little charge fled to the deck, Marianna cast a hurried glance around, in the expectation of seeing her father,—unconscious that she was now an orphan. Naomi's sinking down upon the deck, as we have described, left the child entirely to herself, for a time, and she saw no way of safety, except by following to

the best of her understanding the advice
which had been given her. Instinctively, she
dropped upon her knees, and put her hands
together, as she did when she said her
prayers. As we have mentioned, it was just
day-break, and she still wore her white
night-dress, while her long, fair hair, half un-
curled by the salt spray that was sprinkled
over it, hung loosely down her back.

She did not look at the huge waves that
hurried foaming and roaring, to dash themselves upon the trembling vessel; she did
not look at the torn sails and bending masts,
nor at the sharp rocks amidst which the
schooner was driven. She dreaded to look
anywhere except *"to God;"* and although
but a little child of three years old, who can
doubt that that upward gaze was directed
by a real faith. It was towards a clouded
and stormy sky that Marianna gazed, but

she fully believed that above that sky dwelt
the good and great Being, who was now
looking down at her, and who knew the
confidence that she placed in Him.

Hark, that sudden crash!—One of the
masts has snapped off, and fallen across the
deck, missing but little of striking Naomi,
who starts half up, and clasps Marianna in
her arms. Seeing that the vessel is going
to pieces, Von Ulden also hurries to Marianna, and, with some broken ropes, binds
both her and her nurse securely to the
fallen mast. There is a yet more fearful
crash, as the shattered wreck is hurled upon
the beach. Now, even the sky is hidden
from Marianna by the breakers that dash
over her;—and her eyes, which she has
persistently kept uplifted, amidst so many
dangers and horrors, are forced to close in
blank unconsciousness.

But He to whom Marianna had looked so trustingly, was watching over her, with tender love, and it was not long before she again opened her eyes, and found herself yet in this world. She lay upon a clean though coarse bed, in the principal room of a cottage not far from the beach. The floor was bare, the furniture very plain, and round the walls hung fishing-nets, lanterns, coils of rope, and various things that had belonged to foundered vessels. Two or three women were bending anxiously over Marianna, and when she revived and looked around, exclamations of joy broke from their lips. Naomi lay upon some bed-clothing spread on the floor, for she was still insensible from the effects of the cuts and bruises which she had received, while clasping little Marianna, so as to shield her with her own body from receiving any injury.

2*

The mistress of the cottage gave Marianna a warm kiss, accompanied with the words, "So, my pretty lamb, you are safe, at last!"

"Yes, ma'am,"—answered the child, with all the simplicity of her age, "I kept looking up to God, as long as I could keep my eyes open."

The three women stared at Marianna, and then at each other, with an expression of wonder, not unmixed with *awe*. It was rarely indeed that they heard pious words, even from the lips of grown people, and still less did they expect to hear them from a little child.

"I'm afraid she wont live, after all," murmured the oldest of the women, as she shook her head, with a melancholy expression. Marianna's next words were, "Where is my papa?" "Your *grand*-papa, you mean, my dove," answered the mistress of the cottage. "He was the only one who came to shore alive, 'sides you and your nurse, and he's getting along finely;—only he's swallowed so much salt water. He'll be mighty glad to see *you* doing so well, pretty chick !"

Marianna considered for a moment or two, and then burst into tears, for, young as she was, she now saw the truth, that she was fatherless, as well as motherless.

Two of the women now turned their attention to Naomi, who was presently restored to consciousness, though still in a weak and suffering state. The first movement she made was to clasp her arms over her bosom, as though she held something in them, but, finding that her nursling was no longer in her embrace, she opened her eyes, and gazing wildly around, exclaimed, "Where is my precious child ?"

" Here, Aunt Naomi," cried Marianna, springing from her bed, and throwing her arms around her nurse's neck. Tears of gladness streamed down Naomi's cheeks, as, sinking back, she ejaculated, " Then, Lord, let me live or die, just as it is thy will!"

CHAPTER II.

THE NEW LIVES OF MARIANNA AND HER GRANDFATHER.

AT the time of which we are writing, that part of the coast of Florida on which Von Ulden, his grand-child, and her nurse, had been cast, was inhabited almost entirely by a kind of people called "wreckers," who made a business of securing for themselves everything of the slightest value which could be saved from the wrecks that frequently occurred upon their "sea beat shore." Such an occupation was, not of course, regulated by the rules of honesty, and often led those who followed it to commit the most barbarous acts;—so that it is needless to say they were a very hardened, unprincipled class of people.

When some of these men came to the beach, to see what they could get from the wreck of Von Ulden's vessel, two of them were accompanied by their wives, who usually assisted in gathering up the spoils. But, no sooner did the women see the insensible form of Marianna, as she and her nurse, still clasping each other, lay upon the wet sand, than their rugged hearts were softened by pity.

Von Ulden lay close by, also insensible, and the wife of the wrecker who lived nearest to this spot, insisted that the child, the nurse, and the old man, should all be carried to her cottage. Her husband made no objection, as he had secured for himself Von Ulden's gold watch, and two sea-chests full of clothing; and, even if the owner had known which of the wreckers had taken this property there were no means of compelling its restoration. The plunderers supposed that Von Ulden's

money·must have have been lost in the sea,
—but this was a mistake, as he had a considerable sum safely hidden away in the li-
nings of the clothes which he then had on.

When Von Ulden first recovered from the
effects of his late accident, he was unable to
make up his mind where he should go, or
what he should do. As he took notice of the
wreckers, and the spoils they had collected,
the idea came into his mind that he could
not find any occupation which would suit
him better than to remain where he was, and
become a wrecker himself. Poor Marianna
was too young to understand any thing of
the nature of her grandfather's resolution, or
of the trouble which, at a future day, it was
to cause them both.

Upon a small island, close to the coast,
there stood a half ruined cottage, which the
ignorant people in that vicinity supposed to

be "haunted." Von Ulden, however, very truly observed that there was no danger of his seeing there any worse spirit than himself. He had the cottage enlarged and repaired, after purchasing it, for a trifling sum, from a man who claimed to be its owner; and this place was for many years the home of Marianna.

Von Ulden provided himself with boats and other apparatus, superior to anything owned by the other wreckers, and hired two or three men to assist him in gathering a large share of booty from the wrecks which occurred. This soon excited the jealousy of the other wreckers; but Von Ulden pacified them by making liberal presents to them and their families, and by treating them frequently to spirituous liquors.

At length he proposed that they should form a company, or association, to share equally all the labors, the dangers, and the profits of their business. This was accordingly done, and Von Ulden was appointed the head and director of all the other wreckers, who were accustomed, jokingly, to term him "the Commodore." Here, then, he had everything that he wished for; and we cannot say that his conscience troubled him, for it was daily becoming more and more hardened.

But what satisfaction, what peace of mind, did he enjoy?—Around him were men whom he incited to seize the property of others, and whom he even encouraged to take human life, rather than give up their ill-gotten booty.

How could he feel certain that, some time, they might not rob and murder him?—By night and by day, he always kept a pistol convenient to his hand, and, when the other wreckers were near him, he frequently rolled his eyes around with a look full of suspicion and restlessness.

It is strange how far apart the lives of Marianna and her grandfather seemed to be, though living beneath the same roof! In the little girl's eyes, their new home was beautiful and pleasant. The house was a two story frame building, with two rooms on a floor, separated by a broad hall-way. On one side of the lower hall was a room in which Von Ulden was accustomed to receive the other wreckers, and to settle his accounts with them. Here, there was very little of ordinary furniture, but quite an assortment of wooden chests, piles of sails, ropes, and other things gathered from wrecks. On the opposite side of the hall was the sitting-room, a large and airy apartment, with the floor covered with white and red matting. The mantel-shelf and tables were adorned with beautiful shells, corals, dried sea-plants, and many other curious and pretty things, which had been given to Marianna by her grandfather, or by the wives of the wreckers. One of the apartments up stairs was the sleeping-room of Von Ulden, where he kept the most valuable part of his plunder, carefully locked up. The other was the bed-chamber of Marianna and her nurse.

A white servant woman slept in a room over the kitchen, which was in a small building separate from the main dwelling, according to a common custom in the South. Attached to the house was a garden, nearly filled with orange trees, now growing wild and untended, yet showing many a tempting golden-tinted globe, suspended amidst their dark green leaves.

A cluster of these orange trees, entwined

with flowering vines, formed a charming little bower, where Marianna sat and played.
She was generally alone, while amusing herself, for her grand-father wished her to be
brought up *a lady*, and would rarely allow
her to have anything to say to the rude and
ignorant children of the wreckers. But she
had pet birds and squirrels, and played with
them so often that she and they seemed quite
to understand each other's language.

Sometimes, Marianna would gather different kinds of fruit, and give a feast to her
pets, in the orange tree bower. Her table
was a flat moss-covered stone; her dishes
were acorn-cups, and pink and white shells,
which she picked up on the beach. All her
play-things were gathered from Nature's
great store house.

Marianna's education began by Naomi's
teaching her how to read, which was as far

as her own knowledge extended. To this,
Von Ulden added his instructions in writing
and arithmetic, for he knew that Marianna
could not claim any superiority over the
children of the wreckers, if she was no more
intelligent than they were. But, by far the
most important knowledge which Marianna
ever possessed was conveyed by Naomi; for
she alone gave to the little island girl that
religious instruction which my young readers
receive from parents, Sunday-school teachers,
and pastors. Every day Marianna and her
nurse read the Bible together, especially the
New Testament, and many a long and earnest conversation did they hold concerning
those grand and wonderful truths:—

"How guiltless blood for guilty man was shed,
How he who bore in Heaven the second name
Had not on earth the where to lay his head;
How his first followers and servants sped;
The precepts sage they wrote to many a land;

3*

How he who lone in Patmos banished,
Saw in the sun a mighty angel stand,
And heard great Babylon's doom pronounced by
Heaven's command."

Often, Marianna would address to her
grandfather some artless remarks, that were
like gall and wormwood to a soul so wrapped up in sin. While she was a small child,
Von Ulden heard these remarks in gloomy
silence, or turned the conversation to some
other subject; but as she grew older, he became more impatient upon such occasions.
One afternoon, she was sitting at her grandfather's feet, engaged in tying up bunches of
richly colored wild flowers which she had
gathered upon the island. Von Ulden had
a book in his hand, but soon threw it down,
with a sort of groaning yawn that showed
how hard it was for him to be amused or
satisfied.

"Grandpapa," said Marianna, suddenly

looking up into his face, "I never see you read the Bible!—Sha'nt I get it, and read to you about Jesus, and what He did for us?"

The hardened old man glared upon his innocent grand child like a wild beast that has just felt the cut of the keeper's whip.

"*No!*" was his harsh and angry reply, "I don't want to hear about anything of the kind. It must be old Naomi that fills your head with such stuff, and if there was anybody else here, that could take such good care of you, I'd send her away for putting you up to torment me in this fashion!"

The child grew pale and trembled at her grandfather's look, and, while the tears began to flow down her cheeks, she exclaimed, "Oh grandpapa, don't be angry with Naomi, and I'll never talk to you so again!"

"See that you don't then," was Von Ulden's sharp retort.

Marianna did not dare to speak again to him upon such subjects, but she often thought of the strangeness of her grandfather's conduct, and it seemed to her more and more mysterious.

Naomi was indeed, the only person with whom Marianna could talk freely, and as the little girl grew older, she began to make frequent inquiries about her nurse's former history.—Having been told by Naomi that she had once been a slave, Marianna inquired, "How long since you were set free, aunt Naomi?"

"It's been about fifteen years ago that Mr. Thompson, my Georgia master, gave me my freedom," said Naomi. "But, dear child, I was set free long before *that*. Even while people thought me nothing but a poor slave, the Truth had made me free, and the great King of Glory adopted me for his own child!

My husband and all my children were sold,
—one here, one there,—but all to far-off
places, so that I shall never, never meet
them again, until these eyes open upon the
light of Heaven. But no one could sell my
Saviour away from me! He has been with
me always, though I can't see Him now, for
the veil of mortality that's over my face, but
when I do see him, at last, I shall see my
husband and children too!"

CHAPTER III.

THE passing away of ten years, from the time that they were first ship-wrecked upon the Florida coast, brought about far greater changes in Marianna, her grandfather and her nurse, than in any of the objects around them. Marianna was now thirteen years old, and, though the wreckers and their families often saw the island girl, they always gazed upon her with that wondering reverence which they might have felt upon seeing a spirit from the dwelling place of the blessed. Her hair, (which she still continued to wear in those long and beautiful curls that nature had arranged,) was of rather

35

a light brown color; her eyes were very dark. There was an earnestness, an intensity of expression nothing less than thrilling to the beholder. Her delicate features lighted up with a look so noble, so refined and pure, that the proudest princess on earth could hardly have dared to assume any airs of superiority towards her, in the simple dress of light colored " print," or lawn, which she usually wore. Already, she took the oversight of the household affairs, and was very expert in the use of her needle,—for she was one of those amiable yet energetic characters that never need any driving or urging to make them useful.

Naomi was an elderly woman at the time when we began our narrative, and the addition of ten years made her quite feeble. She herself saw plainly that her health was failing, and, in talking with Marianna, she often endeavored to prepare her for the separation that must soon take place. Marianna only answered by her tears, and by redoubling her care and attention to her nurse's comfort, while she remained with her.

Every clear afternoon, Naomi would take her Bible in one hand, and in the other, the stick she used in walking, and go to a venerable orange tree, that for fifty years had continued to scatter its fragrant blossoms, and bear its sweet, refreshing fruit.

Here, within sight of the ocean, she would sit, and read, and meditate, until night drew near.

One day, when she seemed unusually feeble, Marianna assisted her to reach this favorite spot, and then returned home to see that her grandfather's supper was prepared and served. When the sun was about to set, she hastened back, to assist Naomi in return-

4

ing to the house. She sat leaning against the orange tree, with the Bible in her lap, open at the 21st chapter of Revelations, in which she had been reading a description of the city that is made of gold, and pearl, and all manner of precious stones. In thinking over this description, she had raised her eyes from the book, and, looking across the sea, at the western sky, she saw there a glorious picture, formed by the sunset clouds, that seemed like the golden palaces, and rainbow colored hills, of the heavenly land of which she was meditating. And, as she thus gazed, her spirit passed quickly over land and ocean, and through those glowing clouds, and entered the city of her King !

The placid look, and unclosed eyes of her nurse, prevented Marianna, at first, from seeing what had happened. She came near, and spoke to Naomi. Surprised at receiving no answer she took hold of her hand, but quickly let it fall. At this moment Lucy the white servant, came to tell Marianna that her grandfather was growing impatient at her absence.

"Lucy," cried Marianna, "do come here, to aunt Naomi, and tell me what is the matter with her!" Lucy came up, gazed at the aged woman's lifeless form, touched it, and then shook her head with a significant look.

"Can we do nothing for her?" exclaimed Marianna. "But, look, Lucy,—what are those white wings waving, far out at sea?"

"Why, they must be some kind of sea-birds, of course," answered Lucy, with surprise.

"Oh, no, no," said Marianna, bursting into tears, "they are angels, that are carrying away aunt Naomi!"

The earthly remains of Naomi were laid

to rest beneath the ancient orange tree, whose fruit and blossoms, dropping upon her grave, might well be compared to the good deeds she had done, and to the fragrance of her precious memory.

She had no monument, except in the living virtues of the sweet girl whom she had reared, and no epitaph, except that which was engraved upon the orphan's grateful heart.

Time had reduced Marianna's grandfather to a most unhappy condition. He was now seventy years old, and crippled by the rheumatism to a degree which added much to the infirmities of old age. But this was nothing, compared with the increased harshness and irritability of his temper. A violent, headstrong disposition, which its owner has cherished during a whole lifetime, often seems, in old age, like a sort of insanity:

and Von Ulden might have equalled any of
the Roman tyrants in cruel barbarity, if
Providence had not kindly denied him the
power to do so.

Marianna found it almost impossible to
get any servant to remain with such a master;
and Lucy, though a remarkably good-natured
girl, left them suddenly, one morning, because Von Ulden had thrown a large cup
full of coffee at her head, because the bev-
erage was not quite as strong as he liked it.
As Lucy told everybody the reason of her
leaving, no girl or woman, among the families
of the wreckers, offered to take her place;
and Marianna,— child as she was,—proposed
to her grandfather that she should do all the
house-work herself. But Von Ulden, at this
idea, flew into a terrific passion, and accused
his grand-daughter of wishing to "degrade"
both herself and him, by such "mean-spirited

4*

conduct as that of performing a servant's
duties.

While Marianna was thus perplexed, there
came to the house a poor widow, whose only
son had been drowned. Since this loss, she
had been extremely poor, and only managed
to live at all by assisting the wrecker's wives
in their washing, and other hard work. Of
late, however, she had received a great deal
of assistance from the charity of Marianna,
whose mind was already active in finding out
ways of doing good. This widow gladly
consented to do the chief part of the house-
work in Von Ulden's family. Marianna
promised to see that she was liberally paid,
but apprised her, at the same time, that a
great deal of patience would be required in
waiting upon her grand-father.

"Oh, my dear Miss, was the reply, " I can
stand his crossness, when I think of your

goodness ;—and even if you had promised
me nothing but food and shelter, I should
be glad enough to work for *you !*"

Nothing aggravated Von Ulden so much
as the way in which he was now treated by
the other wreckers. It could scarcely be
expected that they would have enough of
kindness, patience, and delicacy of feeling, to
excuse the " old Commodore's" disagreeable
caprices on account of his age and infirmities.
They had once admired his boldness, shrewd-
ness, and energy; they now despised his
weakness, and considered him no longer of
any importance to them.

The little Island where Von Ulden dwelt
was now deserted, except by himself, his
grand-child, and the woman who worked for
them ;—but this was a source of satisfaction
to Marianna, who had always retreated, as

fast and as far as possible, from seeing and
hearing their wrecker visitors.

Finding that these men no longer came to
him to ask advice, to receive orders, or to
bring a portion of their spoils, Von Ulden
resolved to go to them, and demand the reason of their conduct.

Accordingly with the help of Marianna,
he stepped into a little *batteau*, and a black
boy, who held the oars, quickly rowed him
to the main land. When he came on shore,
the barefooted and bushy-headed children no
longer, as in former days, retired to a distance, and with their fingers in their mouths,
gazed, in awe-struck silence, at "the Commodore." They followed him, laughing and
hooting, and, when the angry old man turned
around, and endeavored to strike some of
them with his stick, they ran off a little way,

and then returned, with louder laughter than before.

"Look at the old Alligator," cried one of these rude urchins, comparing Von Ulden's useless anger to that of the animal mentioned, who, however he may wish to turn short upon his pursuers, or his intended prey, is always too clumsy to do so.

Seeing a couple of women standing in the doors of the two nearest cottages, Von Ulden began to scold them for allowing their children to be so insolent, but they in return, scolded him with such shrillness and volubility that he was soon forced to give up the contest. He then addressed himself to some of the men, who were lounging about, smoking their pipes, and, in a harsh, imperious manner, demanded to know why it was that he had not seen anything of them for so long? But the wreckers only turned him into ridicule, and laughed at his assumed authority over them.

"None of your tantrums, Commodore," said one fellow,—"you've got to be an old broken up hulk, now, and fit for nothing but fire-wood."

"Yes," added another, "we've cut you adrift now, Dad, and you may as well float along quietly, until your crazy timbers land in Davy Jones's locker!"

Von Ulden found that to threaten and denounce these ruffians only increased their contemptuous mirth, and he was perfectly helpless to avenge himself. He turned away, and hobbled to his boat again, while some of the children, encouraged by the insolence of their parents, pelted him with hand-fulls of sand.

When Von Ulden returned home, he threw himself into an arm-chair, and his long gray beard flowed down over his breast, as he dropped his head forward, in utter abandonment to misery. Not one ray of the divine philosophy of the Gospel was there, to soothe and control the unutterable tortures of a fierce and haughty spirit, suffering under a foul insult, for which it is utterly powerless to obtain any redress. Yet Von Ulden would not, for a moment, entertain the thought that all this shame, and wretchedness, and desolation, were the fruits of his own conduct. He had chosen to cast in his lot with the wicked, and here was the natural result.

Marianna was too intelligent and observing a girl not to surmise, pretty clearly, the cause of her grandfather's present distress. "What a pity, what a sorrowful pity, it is, that he ever had anything to do with these men," she thought to herself; but she dared not say so, lest Von Ulden should consider

it, as a hint that he himself was to blame for
his sad situation. She longed to say something that would comfort him, but there was
in his disposition so much that she could not
understand, and so much that she feared, as
to render the task a difficult one indeed.

Presently, she approached him timidly,
and, in the softest of her soft tones said,
"Grandpapa, I'm sure it would make you
feel better if you were to *pray* a little."

Von Ulden, at this suggestion, felt very
much like a criminal who, when his guilt is
detected and he tries to seek safety in flight
and concealment, is advised by some friend
to take shelter in a court of justice. He
raised his head, stared at Marianna with
angry astonishment, and then uttered a curse
upon her "folly."

"Begone from my sight, this moment,"

said he, " and learn better than to aggravate my troubles by your impudent advice !"

There was nothing left for poor Marianna except sadly to retire from the apartment, and then, in solitude, to pray for him who thus obdurately refused to seek God's mercy for himself. She did not pray that the wreckers might be led to treat her grand-father differently, or that he might be given the strength and fortitude of mind not to trouble himself about their contemptuous treatment. All her supplication on his account were for this one thing—that the Lord would so open her grand-father's eyes, and touch his heart, that he might have no grief except for his past sins, and might long for no gain except those riches of God which are laid up in Christ Jesus.

5

CHAPTER IV.

IT might certainly seem that, after
Naomi's death, Marianna was left in
a very lonesome and melancholy condition; and so, indeed it would have been,
but for one source of comfort, which could
never die. Marianna could not tell the exact
hour when she became a Christian, for, by
the teachings of her good nurse, the name of
Jesus was blended with her earliest recollec-
tions. As she grew older, and more thoughtful, she felt a warmer appreciation of his
wondrous love, and a deeper conviction of
her need of the Saviour. Having so little
of human companionship, she came to hear,
with wonderful distinctness, the voice of

God conversing with her soul, both through the pages of the Bible, and the scenes of nature. Her pleasures were pure and simple, and she knew nothing of the feverish excitements, or the perilous temptations, of theatres and ball-rooms. While attending to her flowers, feeding her birds, or rambling along the sea-beach, nothing could be more natural than that thoughts of grateful devotion should arise in her heart, and bring with them some foretaste of the joys of Heaven. Nor did Marianna's life lack the two elements of *usefulness* and *self-sacrifice* which serve both to show the existence of true Christianity in the soul, and to promote its growth there. There was ample room for the exercise of these qualities in attending to her grand-father's comfort, bearing with his peevishness, and endeavoring to soothe the gloom and irritation of his mind.

Of course, she greatly missed her good nurse, and in order to give new employment to her thoughts, she went about the house arranging almost everything which it contained and which she was able to move. While so doing, she found some old books stowed away in an obscure closet, and eagerly examined them; for she had never yet seen any printed volume except a Bible, a hymn book, and an arithmetic.

The books which she discovered were a large and handsomely illustrated geography, and three or four works upon ancient and modern history. Every word in each one of these volumes was intently studied and eagerly devoured by her, for she longed to know something about those mysterious lands which formed the other shore of that broad ocean upon which, each day, her gaze was accustomed to rest. My young readers who

5*

are blessed with so many advantages, will doubtless smile at the island-girl's simplicity; but, in studying these books, she felt as though she was drinking in knowledge at a thousand inlets, and it seemed to her that she could feel the scales of ignorance falling from her eyes.

No new-found treasures, however, could lessen her love for the oldest, truest, sweetest book of all. On a certain memorable day she took her Bible and went down to the shore. It was late in the afternoon, and her grand-father was lying down, inclined to sleep away as much as possible of the time which hung heavily upon his hands. Marianna took her seat upon a fragment of rock close to the pebbly strand, and shaded by the drooping branches of a magnificent willow tree. If she turned her head to the right or left, she saw the calm and bright expanse of ocean, spreading away to the very horizon, while the little island rested upon its azure bosom like a tiny cloud amidst the clear blue of heaven. Looking straight ahead, she saw the adjacent main-land, stretching out its long line of sea beach, covered with sand of such dazzling whiteness, that it attracts the attention of every stranger who approaches the coast of Florida.

A little farther back, there were scattered, here and there, the rude cottages of the wreckers, and beyond these again appeared trees and bushes, rich green grass and little patches of cultivated ground. Marianna was just near enough to see distinctly the wreckers themselves, some of whom were idling along the beach, some repairing or examining their little boats, and others spreading their fishing nets out in the 'sun. After gazing upon this scene for a short time, she opened her book, and gave her whole attention to its contents. She had not read very long when a loud yet cheerful female voice was heard; "Halloo, Miss Marianna !— Fond of reading, ain't you? Well, it may be pretty work for them that understands it."

A small boat was approaching the shore, rowed by a stoutly built young woman, with a sun-burnt, but good-humored and rather handsome countenance. As she spoke, she touched the island shore and laying down one of her oars, held up a string of fine fish.

"Good afternoon, Mrs. Clarke; I see you have got some nice fish for us as usual" said Marianna, smiling.

"Yes, but don't pay me for 'em now; I want to have something in bank, to get Christmas presents for my husband and the young ones. ' Did you hear the news to-day, about that yacht and them that were on board of her?"

"No," answered Marianna, "we have not heard anything new. Did the yacht strike on a reef?"

"No, bless you, the pilot had to run her ashore, on purpose!"

"Why, what was the matter?"

"Well, it seems that the four sailors who were the crew of this yacht, had agreed to mutiny, and take the vessel, but the cabin boy let out all about it to the owner and commander, Lieutenant Ferrand. So the Lieutenant fastened three of the men down in the hold, and held a pistol to the other one's head, and made him run the yacht ashore, right here. The Lieutenant, the pilot and the cabin boy, got safely through the breakers, but the three men in the hold were drowned.

"Oh, dreadful!" exclaimed Marianna, "Would no one save them?"

"Why, you see, our men were so busy picking up things that had been washed overboard, and were floating around, that they hadn't time to listen to Lieutenant Ferrand. He, as soon as he got breath and strength enough, after getting to shore, shouted to them to save the three sailors down in the hold; but, as I said, our men did'nt stop to pay any attention to him. When they went on board the half-sunk vessel to see what they could find there, they came across the three drowned bodies. My husband got this silver ring from the finger of one of them."

Marianna looked at the speaker with painful wonder, and then to change the subject, said, "I am glad that there were three saved, anyhow."

" Well, that's the queerest part of it," continued Mrs. Clark, unconscious of her listener's emotions at what she had just heard.

" The man they had had for a pilot turned out to be Jack Ross, who lived here for so long, and only went away six or eight months ago. Ross always was one of the hardest cases around here. Among the things that were saved out of the water was Lieutenant Ferrand's chest with all his money in it, and all his clothes, except what he had on. Ross said _he_ must have that, because, if it hadn't been for his getting up the mutiny, the yacht wouldn't have been run ashore here at all, and our men wouldn't have had any pickings off of her. But Ferrand himself stepped up, and drew a pistol, and said the chest was _hi_ , and whoever meddled with it, would do so at his peril. Then Ross jumped on him as if he'd tear him to pieces, and when the

Lieutenant found that Ross would get the best of him, he just shot Jack with the pistol that he had in his hand. Ross dropped like a stone, and was dead in a minute. Does it scare you to hear such things, Miss Marianna? you look pale."

"It was an awful way to die!" sighed Marianna.

"Yes, and our men were *awful mad* about having an old comrade killed that way. They were going to hang Ferrand to the nearest tree, and had got a rope ready noosed, when the cabin boy fell on his knees, and begged them to stop. That just struck them dumb, for I forgot to tell you that this boy was Jack Ross's own son Hugh! While they were wondering what next, old Giles came up, and he too thought the boy acted very strange considering Ferrand had just shot his father; but to hear how the young

scamp cried and begged, you'd have thought
it was a father's life he was pleading for.
Old Giles is always for going *slow and sure*,
and so he persuaded them to keep Lieutenant
Ferrand shut up in an empty hut until to-
morrow morning, and let our men all talk
the matter over, this evening, and make up
their minds what to do with him. But,
Laws!—how long I've been stopping to talk!
I must hurry home, now, and get my husband's supper.—Good bye, Miss Marianna."

Marianna leaned her arm upon her Bible,
and her head upon her hand. She cast her
eyes across the same beautiful prospect of
ocean and land which she had viewed with
so much satisfaction, scarcely half an hour
before,—but a cloud now seemed to rest upon its charms. There was the same blight
that came upon the bloom of Eden after the
fall of man;—there was the darkening and

6

oppressive shade of sin! We cannot wonder that, on contrasting God's works with man's ways, the infidel Rousseau exclaimed, "Inquire no longer, man, who is the author of evil,—behold him in yourself!—Take away all that is the work of man, and all the rest is good." In thinking over what she had just heard from Mrs. Clark, Marianna's reflections were, "God has filled this place with warmth, brightness, beauty, and perfume. Human beings have filled it with strife and misery, wickedness and horror! But how different would things be, if all or most of those here had, by faith in Jesus, received from the Holy Spirit the gift of a new heart!"

It will be remembered that Marianna had never lived in, nor even seen, a really Christian community,—one where the Bible is read, public worship is held, and the professed followers of the Saviour dwell. But her Testament clearly taught her that " The fruit of the Spirit is love, joy, peace, long-suffering, gentleness, goodness, faith, meekness, temperance." She knew that such a scene of heartlessness, plunder and violence, as she had just heard described, could never occur among those whose souls were filled with Christian charity and Christian love.

Then came the thought, "Can the religion of Jesus ever become generally known and loved in this place?" To Marianna it did not appear that such a thing was *impossible*, for here, again, from the pages of her Testament came a silent reply, telling her that the power of God had done even greater things than this. But, as to the manner in which such a wonderful change might be effected, she could not even form a surmise. She could not imagine that it would be in any degree owing to such a feeble instrument as herself. Marianna had no idea that these things of which she had just heard—this plundered vessel, this slaughtered man, this unfortunate prisoner, this son pleading for the slayer of his father,—were but the first links in a chain of incidents which should make plain to her the way in which she was to work for Jesus among the wreckers of Florida.

Here we will leave Marianna, for awhile, to her thoughtful musings, while we sketch the portraits of the new characters just introduced. Children, and ignorant people of all ages, judge of things chiefly by their outside appearance;—and, no doubt, this had something to do with the idolatry, (for it was nothing less,) of young Hugh Ross, towards his late commander, Lieutenant Ferrand. It had also some influence upon the minds of the wreckers,—though even they would have been ashamed to confess such a weakness.

Francis Ferrand had lived thirty-three years, but, (except his faithful term in the Navy) not to do much service. His personal appearance was unusually interesting. His fine features bore an expression of more than ordinary intelligence, combined with frankness and sincerity of disposition, and they were lighted up by a pair of bright, penetrating eyes.

It may easily be judged that now, as he laid himself down upon a rude wooden bench in the otherwise unfurnished hut, he did not look quite as usual. His thick dark hair, and even his moustache, were still damp with seawater; and the light brown, with which a sailor's life had overspread his complexion, had given way to a paleness which showed that neither mind nor body were well. His

6*

head ached from a blow which one of the
wreckers had given him with an oar-blade,
immediately after the shooting of Ross, and
his heart ached from several different causes.
He knew that his life was in great peril from
the ruffians who had him completely in their
power; and he had awaiting him at home, a
lovely and amiable young wife and an infant
daughter. These dear and helpless creatures
would, by his death, be left without any de-
pendence, except upon the charity of others,
for Ferrand, though born to a large fortune,
had, long since, got rid of it. His habits
had not been exactly vicious, though blame-
ably extravagant, and his unbounded generosity, while it really did good to many a de-
serving object, was often used by base and
dishonest persons, to their own advantage.
Now, he could not leave his family enough
to support them for a year,—but this thought

was not needed to give bitterness to the idea of never seeing them again.

It was a painful reflection too, that this unlucky voyage had obliged him, without intending it, to cause the death of all four of the men who had composed the crew of his yacht. The yacht itself, which the wreckers were then plundering,—was the last and most cherished fragment of former wealth and luxury, but Ferrand did not think of that.

Hugh Ross took the first opportunity of speaking aside with old Giles, and requesting that he might be allowed to carry Lieutenant Ferrand a dry suit of clothes from his chest. This was willingly granted, and Giles contrived that Hugh should take the clothes without being seen by any of the other wreckers.

When Hugh entered the hut where Lieu-

tenant Ferrand was confined, he found him
stretched upon the rough wooden bench, as
we have described. His eyes were closed,
one arm was beneath his head, and the other
hand rested upon the back of the bench.
Hitherto, Hugh had seen him unconquerably
active, lively and hopeful. He had seen him
surrounded by men who were obliged to
treat him with the utmost deference, and to
obey every word that he uttered. Now, how
forlorn, melancholy and helpless was his situation!

Tears filled the boy's eyes;—he approached
softly, took the hand that rested upon the
bench-back, and pressed it to his lips. Lieutenant Ferrand immediately unclosed his
eyes, and was not surprised at seeing Hugh,
for he had recognized his cabin-boy's step as
soon as he entered. But—for reasons which
the reader will soon understand—he felt as

though he would rather not look at him. However, the Lieutenant was surprised by Hugh's action, and gazed at him in silence for a moment or two, while three or four different expressions passed, by turns, over his countenance. He then said, in a tone of rebuke, "Boy, did you not see your father fall by my hand, not more than an hour ago?"

Hugh became of a deathly paleness, and answered in a choked voice, "Yes sir,—but I know you could'nt help it."

"Very true," replied Ferrand, with no less sterness than before, "but, whatever his character may have been, John Ross was still *your father*, and it does not become you to kiss the hand that killed him."

So pointed and unexpected a rebuke from such a quarter, completely destroyed what yet remained of Hugh's self-possession. He hastily laid the bundle of clothing down at

Lieutenant Ferrand's feet, then turned away, buried his face in his hands, and, sobbing convulsively, left the hut. As soon as he could regain enough outward calmness, he repaired to the cottage of old Giles, where the wreckers were now assembling, to decide the question of their prisoner's life or death.

Samuel Giles was the oldest man in the wrecker community, but at the age of sixty, he was still strong and active. During the greater part of his life he had been a sailor in the U. S. Navy, and had borne a good character. But the temptations of bad company and bad example at length overcame him, and brought him to adopt a wrecker's calling. As Giles always dealt fairly by his comrades, and was never known to break his word, the other wreckers felt as much respect for him as such men could feel for one of their own crew, and they had lately

urged him to become their head, or " Commodore," in the place of Von Ulden. But
Giles was the son of pious, though humble
parents, and would doubtless have become a
Christian himself, if he had not, when a
mere youth, forsaken his home and its influ-
ences, to run away to sea. Often, now, when
engaged with his fellow-wreckers in some
act of heartless robbery, there would flash
across Giles' mind the remembrance of a
mothers' prayers and a father's godly coun-
sels, and his stalwart frame shivered at the
fear of a judgment to come. Yet this man,
who had faced so many dangers, had not the
moral courage to say anything against the
lawless conduct of his associates, or to de-
cline following the same mode of life. He
therefore made all sorts of feigned excuses
for not taking the leadership of the wreckers,
and cherished in his heart the delusive hope

that God would be bribed by this piece of self-denial, to overlook his daily transgressions.

CHAPTER V.

S one crime naturally leads to another, those wreckers who had appropriated the largest share of Lieutenant Ferrand's property were now anxious to have him put to death. The pretext which they gave for this was a desire to avenge the death of John Ross, but every one knew that they really opposed Ferrand's being set at liberty because they feared that he might bring them into trouble for their acts of robbery. Hugh Ross listened, with anxious emotion, to the hardened and merciless speeches now made by these men, one of whom concluded his argument by saying,

(78)

"Jack Ross was one of ourselves,—as you may say,—but who knows or cares anything about *this* chap?"

"*I* do," boldly answered Hugh.

"Well," rejoined the preceding speaker, "you ought to be ashamed of yourself to say so! If *I* had a son that would'nt avenge my death, nor even want it avenged, I'd break every bone in his body!"

"Never mind," observed old Giles, "talking don't cost anything, nor listening, neither. So, go on, Hugh, and say all that you want to."

The wreckers did not require any introduction to tell them who this boy was. His history is briefly this:

John Ross and his wife had always been noted in their community as a quarrelsome and disorderly couple, and both were frequently known to be intoxicated. Their

eldest son had been killed in a dispute with
another wrecker, and the second was drowned
while endeavoring to secure his share of
plunder from a sinking vessel. But these
losses did not render Hugh's parents any
more gentle and affectionate towards their
surviving child. Mrs. Ross,—as might have
been expected from such a woman, possessed
very little tender feeling, but what natural
affection she had, was often roused to protect
her child from the brutal ill-treatment of
Ross. He was surly and disagreeable, and,
when anything provoked him, he yielded to
every suggestion that the author of mischief
could breathe into a wicked heart.

Hugh knew no more about books and
learning than do the sparrow's young, or
the fox's cubs; and what is far worse, he
knew nothing at all about religion. He had
never seen a Bible,—never uttered or heard

uttered a prayer, and knew his Creator's
name only from hearing it in oaths and curses.
Thus, until he was twelve years old, Hugh
had led a life which might very well have
been compared to that of a neglected and
ill-treated dog. At the age of twelve, he
lost his mother, and this would have made
his condition worse than ever, if some of his
mother's relations, who were decent people,
residing in Tallahassee, had not accidentally
heard of his miserable situation. His father
made not the slightest objection to letting
him go to Tallahassee; indeed, he was glad
to get rid of him. By means which we need
not stop to relate, his mother's relatives contrived to have Hugh placed on board of a
man-of-war, as one of the ship's boys; and,
for three years past, nothing had been seen
or heard of him by the wrecker community.
When he left that community, Hugh was a

thin puny, half-starved child;—but he now
appeared as a stout, ruddy-cheeked boy,
with the resolute look of one who had become accustomed to thinking and acting for
himself.

On Giles now giving him leave to speak,
Hugh proceeded, as concisely as he could, to
relate his own history, since leaving Florida.

During his first voyage on a man-of-war,
nothing had made such an impression on his
mind as the great social distance between the
naval officers and those who, like himself,
held the humblest positions on board. It
seemed to him, at first, the natural and
proper state of things for those grand gentlemen in blue broadcloth and gilt buttons,
to act imperiously and insolently towards
the poor, "common," human beings who appeared to have no mission in life except to
obey their orders. But soon, he noticed that

one of these gentlemen, and that one, the
most elegant, and truly dignified of them all,
never swore, nor vociferated, nor used rough
or abusive language. Lieutenant Ferrand
became, at once, the poor sailor boy's ideal
of human perfection ; and he even had the
daring ambition, (as it seemed to himself,) to
"wish that his Maker had made *him* such a
man."

One day, while talking with a boy who
was his intimate associate, Hugh thoughtfully
observed, " I wonder if a boy that has been
brought up like me, could ever get to be a
real *gentleman ?*"

Lieutenant Ferrand overheard this remark,
and was pleased with the spirit of it. "My
lad," said he to Hugh, "if you ever wish to
raise yourself, you must begin by trying to
know more than you do now."

Hugh caught eagerly at this suggestion,

coming from a source which he so highly esteemed. Encouraged by Lieutenant Ferrand,
he learned first to read and then to write,
having persuaded one of the ship's boys, who
had received a decent education, to assist him
in his studies. Ferrand praised Hugh's
quickness in learning, and pointed out various
needful improvements in his manners and
habits, which Hugh adopted with a prompt-
ness that still farther increased the Lieutenant's good opinion of him. Young Ross now
became neat and cleanly in his appearance,
left off swearing, and the use of coarse and
vicious expressions, and gave every proof of
having been stimulated to en'er upon an
honorable career.

The three years' cruise was very nearly
over, when a sailor, one day, trod on the
paw of the Captain's dog, and made him
limp. On being taxed with this grave of-

fence, the man was frightened, and laid it
upon Hugh. Without listening to the boy's
denial, the enraged despot of the ship
knocked him down, and kicked and tramp-
led on him in his fury. Lieutenant Ferrand
was not far off, and hastening up, he seized
the Commander by the arm, jerked him away
from Hugh, and indignantly expressed his
opinion of the cruelty and unmanliness of
such conduct. The Captain, who had always
imagined himself to be "lord of all he sur-
veyed," was astounded by this bold interfer-
ence, but no revenge which he could have
taken *on the spot*, was sufficient to satisfy his
insulted dignity. So, as he walked away to
his own cabin, he merely said to Ferrand
with a menacing air, "You shall be made
sorry for this, sir!"

A few days afterwards, when the vessel
entered the port of New York, Lieutenant

Ferrand was put under arrest and tried by a
Court Martial for his disrespect to his Commander. He made no attempt to deny or
explain away the charge, and was sentenced
to be "suspended" for a long period, from
the U. S. service. Immediately after the
trial was over, Hugh Ross saw the Lieutenant, who said to him, with a smile full of
lofty feeling, "Hugh, I'm *not sorry yet !*"

Hugh, however, was sorry to the very
soul, in thinking what a return he had,
though innocently and unintentionally,—
made for all Ferrand's kindness and conde-
scension. *He*, too, obtained his discharge
from the Navy, and, for some time afterwards
picked up a precarious living by doing odd
jobs of work about the streets of New York
city. One day, he accidentally met with
Lieutenant Ferrand, who since his suspension from the Navy, had been doing nothing

in particular. His relatives, and those of his
wife, had offered him the choice of several
good situations, in large mercantile houses,
but he declined to take any of them, as all
his early training and habits had disqualified
him for such a position.

He had now purchased from a friend the
right of a patent, *spice-grinding* machine,
with which he was about to make a voyage
of speculation to the West Indies, in his own
yacht. On meeting Hugh, he at once engaged him as his cabin-boy, and then adver-
tised for a few seamen to serve as crew.
Among the men who presented themselves
was John Ross. As soon as Lieutenant
Ferrand learned that he was Hugh's Father,
he accepted him without asking for any
other recommendation. Ross evinced no gladness, or emotion of any kind, at the unexpected meeting with his son, and Hugh's de-

meanor still showed the force of that habit
which, ever since infancy, had taught him to
shun and to fear a father's presence.

During their voyage to the West Indies,
Lieutenant Ferrand treated Hugh with a
more marked kindness than ever, as if to
show that he bore no grudge for the boy's
having been the unfortunate occasion of his
suspension from the Navy. What Hugh
esteemed the greatest favor, was being allowed access to his Commander's small but
select library of choice books, in which the
cabin-boy found a gold-mine of new ideas.

These were days of sunshine, but a shadow
was drawing nigh. The patent spice-mill
proved a failure which did not even pay the
expenses of the trip;—and we have already
seen how disastrously the homeward voyage was interrupted. "And now," said
Hugh, in conclusion, "I don't know how

anybody can blame me for not wanting to see Lieutenant Ferrand hanged. You need not take his life to get what belongs to him either, for if you let him go free, and he promises not to put you to any trouble, I can tell you that he will never be worse than his word."

Here Hugh concluded his story, to which the wreckers had listened with remarkable patience. Nothing was said until each of them had taken another drink of spirits and water, and then old Giles began thus:

"You've heard this boy's speech,—and now hear mine. You want somebody to be your commander, in place of Von Ulden, but I'm not the kind of man you need. I'm too old, and too stupid. We've all seen that Lieutenant Ferrand is a brave man, and Hugh's story shows that he's good-natured and whole-souled. Besides, he knows more than any of us, or he couldn't have held the position that he did, in the Navy. I've been too long in the service myself, not to have it cut pretty deeply into my mind that a navy officer, as a general thing, has to be something more than common.—How much finer Commodore he would be for us than Von Ulden!"

The wreckers were evidently struck by this idea, but, after a pause, one of them remarked, " There's always two sides to a bargain, though ; and, even if we are willing, who knows but that he mightn't be ?"

" I should think he'd like it better than hanging, if the choice were put to him," said another.

"Yes," added Giles, " and just now, when he's suspended from his position in the Navy, and his speculation in the West Indies has failed, and he has lost so much by coming

8

ashore here, I guess he's not in the humor to stand much on ceremony. We'll have a talk with him about it."

Among the listeners to this discussion was a black boy named Peter, who, every day, carried in his little boat to Von Ulden's island, various kinds of meat and vegetables, for the family there to purchase.

At an early hour, next morning, Peter got into his boat and proceeded to the island, with some provisions. While he was disposing of these articles to the servant woman, the talkative young trader told her the latest news, in the shape of Lieutenant Ferrand's capture, and the discussion as to whether he should be put to death, or appointed "Commodore" of the wreckers. This account was listened to with interest, not only by the person to whom it was addressed, but also by Marianna and her grandfather, who were sitting at a couple of open windows, enjoying the sweet freshness of the morning air. Marianna was much relieved in mind to hear that the unfortunate stranger was still alive, and that his life was likely to be spared; but her grandfather felt galled beyond endurance at the very idea of that stranger's being chosen by the wreckers as their chief.

It was plain to Marianna that he was fearfully agitated, but she could imagine very little of his feelings. Presently he said, " Marianna, get your hat on and let Peter row you to the main-land. I have a message that I can send by you only."

Marianna, accordingly, put on her wide-brimmed straw hat, which every time that she wished to wear it, was trimmed anew, by twining about its crown a wreath of fresh flowers, to which she sometimes added one or two pendant pieces ot delicate vines. She then presented herself before her grandfather, to receive his commands.

Von Ulden tried to speak calmly and reasonably, but he shook from head to foot with direful emotions, as he thus addressed Marianna:—"Go to some of the wreckers;—tell them that Von Ulden now sends them the best advice that he ever gave. I have certainly lived long enough, and seen enough of the world to make my counsel of some value, and these men were once glad to ask for it. Tell them, I say that Von Ulden's last advice is, to hang the man who is now their prisoner."

Marianna started back, and vainly tried for a moment or two, to think that she had misunderstood the old man's words.

"Why, grandfather, what has he done?" she presently inquired.

"Don't question me!—don't argue with me! cried Von Ulden, frantically, "Carry the message I have given you."

"Oh, grandfather I—I cannot!" said Marianna, shuddering.

It was now Von Ulden's turn to be astonished, when, for the first time, he found his will resisted by his gentle and dutiful grandchild. A look of agony was blended with the indignation that darkened his features, as he exclaimed, "And you, too, have turned against me!—Now there is not one, —not one being upon earth who will obey this weak voice, or fear the old man's anger! You cannot go indeed! Tell the truth at once, girl, and say that you *will* not."

Marianna was silent. Her good nurse, Naomi, had always taken care to impress upon her mind the beauty and value of obedience,—that virtue which parents are most

8*

delighted to find in their children; and which is the most pleasing tribute that our heavenly Father can receive from his creatures, since it affords the sweetest proof of a true faith in Him. Disobedience to parents is now fully admitted to be that sin which more than all others put together, leads young people to wretchedness and ruin. It was the crime of disobedience committed by the first of human race that "brought Death into the world, and all our woe!"

CHAPTER VI.

MARIANNA OBEYS HER GRANDFATHER'S COM-
MANDS.—LIEUTENANT FERRAND MAKES A
TERRIBLE MISTAKE.—CONVERSATION
BETWEEN HUGH AND MARIANNA.

MARIANNA was now in one of these perplexing situations in which it seemed impossible to escape something very disagreeable. Her greatest anxiety was to choose, not the most pleasant course, but that which was strictly the right one. Her conclusion was, " I will obey my grandfather, and, at the same time, beseech God to preserve me from causing the wreckers to commit another crime, and this poor stranger to loose his life."

It was a strengthening thought, and Marianna was now enabled to answer with out-

ward calmness, "Forgive me, grandfather;
I will go."

"And you will really carry the message I
have given you?" said Von Ulden, not knowing how to account for her sudden change of
manner.

"Yes sir," answered Marianna, looking
into her grandfather's face, while he scanned
her countenance with a searching eye. Von
Ulden had never known his granddaughter
to be guilty of falsehood or deception, and
harsh and suspicious as he was,—he felt that
he had no right to doubt her now. Accordingly he said only, "Go then," and Marianna departed.

She took a seat in Peter's little boat, and
while the boy was rowing her towards the
mainland, her heart was lifted up to God in
silent prayer. She soon stepped on shore,
with a resolution to deliver her message

only to Giles, whom she had discovered to be more human than the other wreckers, and who, therefore, would be less likely to take the advice which she unwillingly conveyed.

As Marianna had no share in her grand-father's unpopularity, she met with no unpleasant demonstrations, upon landing. On the contrary, the men touched their hats as she passed them, and one of the wrecker's wives, meeting her with a smile, said, " Well, my pretty little lady, can any one here do anything for you ?"

" Thank you, ma'am ;—I should like to say something to Mr. Giles, if he is here," replied Marianna.

The woman showed her where Giles was standing, just outside the hut where Lieutenant Ferrand was confined, and before entering which, he was studying how to open the delicate and important conversation that he

was to hold with the prisoner. The sound
of Marianna's voice roused Giles from his
meditations, and he greeted her with, "Good
morning, Miss Marianna;—it's an uncom-
mon treat to see *you* here, and so early
in the morning too!"

"The truth is, Mr. Giles," said she, speaking with a great effort,—"grandfather insisted
upon my coming here, to bring the wreckers
his last advice,—as he says, and that advice
is that—that you will hang the man whom
you have now got prisoner!"

Here Marianna was so much shocked by
the sound of her own words that she turned
pale, and was unable to say anything more.
Giles, however, seemed to think her grandfather's message a very characteristic one.
In reply, he merely shrugged his shoulders,
lifted his grizzly eye-brows, and put a quid
of tobacco into his mouth. The old sailor

then proceeded to unfasten and open the door of the hut before which they stood, and, looking in, he said, with a grim smile, " Good morning, Lieutenant. Here's a young lady come to say that the best thing we can do is to hang you."

Lieutenant Ferrand had been walking slowly back and forth, for want of something else to do, but he now stopped near the open door, and looked at Marianna in extreme amazement. He would have thought it cause enough for surprise to see a creature so delicately fair, in this wild place, and amidst these rude and lawless people, but to hear that this lovely child wished to have the unfortunate stranger put to a horrible death,—was indeed a subject of the greatest wonder.

We need not say that Marianna was most painfully confused, and the color which had been entirely banished from her face, some

minutes before, now came rushing back in
one flow of crimson. Unable to bear the
idea of being so misunderstood, she hastily
exclaimed, "It was not I who thought so;—
It was my grandfather!"

"Indeed?" said Lieutenant Ferrand, smiling, "and what have I done to the old gentleman, that he wishes to see me strangled?"

"You would'nt ask that if you knew him,
Lieutenant," answered Giles. "I don't know
how even this young lady can have patience
with such a grandfather, for he's one of the
most outrageous old,—"

"Wait a moment Mr. Giles,"—said Marianna, with dignity, "I am going away now,
and then you can talk of my grandfather as
you choose."

So saying, she walked rapidly away, re-en-
tered Peter's boat, and was rowed back to
the island.

Giles satisfied Lieutenant Ferrand's curiosity, by giving a brief account of Marianna and her grandfather, and then proceeded to speak of the subject which was uppermost in his mind that morning. Strange as it may seem, Giles could perceive that he himself would not do right in becoming the leader of the wreckers, and yet he could reconcile it with his conscience to persuade a younger and more experienced person to do this very thing! The old sailor imagined that, in this way, he was shifting the moral responsibility from himself to Lieutenant Ferrand :—and all that we can say to explain or excuse these ideas is that Giles had very dim and cloudy notions of what Christianity really consists. He commenced the conversation by asking Lieutenant Ferrand if he had any family; and, when the Lieutenant replied that he had a wife and child, Giles saw his breast give a

9

short quick heave, that told of smothered
emotions.

Giles then proceeded to say that he was
afraid the wreckers would never consent to
spare their prisoner's life, except upon one
condition. What that condition was, our
readers know already, but Lieutenant Ferrand was very much surprised on hearing it,
and it was plainly to be seen from his countenance, that he felt himself highly affronted.
His face flushed as he exclaimed, " And do
these thieving vagabonds really imagine that
I would be their leader ?   Your people have
taken my vessel, my money, and almost
everything that I possessed besides, and now
do they think to rob me even of my honesty
and respectability ?"

Giles did not think it at all strange that
Lieutenant Ferrand should view the matter

in this light, and yet he tried to look as if he did consider it singular.

"Well sir," said he, "I am only anxious to save your life,—especially as you have a family. But, I suppose, if anything should happen to you, they would be well provided for. I dare say, your relations, or your lady's relations, are well off and some of them might,—"

"I want none of their help, for my family or myself," hastily answered Ferrand.

The fact is, that the manner in which the Lieutenant had allowed his large fortune to slip through his fingers,—the way in which he had incurred a suspension from his position in the Navy, and the visionary and unprofitable speculations which he had since been trying, had caused all of his wife's relations and most of Ferrand's own, to declare that he was not capable of taking care of himself, much less of a family. They expressed great pity for Mrs. Ferrand, but she always disclaimed the idea of being a fit subject for compassion, and assured her husband's detractors that they would yet see him pursuing a useful and prosperous career. Now, Ferrand thought when he returned home from another unsuccessful speculation, and plundered of everything, how painful would be the feeling of his devoted Blanche, and how keen the sneers of her relations.

He was silent, and Giles thus continued to speak :—" There's no mistake about it that a great deal is to be made by this business, if it is carried on by a man of sense and spirit. Old Von Ulden made enough, while he was at it, to keep himself and his granddaughter comfortable all their lives. What I thought, sir, was that you might promise to be our " Commodore" just for one year, and reserve the liberty, after that, to keep the situation or not, just as you choose. Then sir, when that time is up, you might go home full-handed, and nobody you care for, need know exactly what business you had been in."

Lieutenant Ferrand began to feel that there was some temptation in this, but though shaken, he was not conquered.

In a low yet resolute voice, he answered, "I was not trained for any such life as this. I have some conscience, and value principle far more than money."

At these words, Giles himself turned pale, and those horrors of conscience to which, at times, he was subject, came suddenly over him. Yet still,—with the fatal obstinacy that ruins so many souls, he would not yield to the conviction that he was utterly a sinner, and had no hope but in God's pardoning

9*

grace. On the contrary, he cast about in his mind for some excuse that should justify his present conduct in his own opinion, as well as in Lieutenant Ferrand's.

Presently, his brow cleared up, and with a new confidence, Giles thus began to speak: " Well, the fact is, Lieutenant, I wasn't trained for this kind of thing neither. My parents were good people, and tried to teach me what was right, and now, that I'm getting old, I often feel that I would like to lead a different life. Now, most of the wreckers, here, don't seem to know right from wrong, and I think that, if they had a leader that they would respect and obey, and that had a conscience of his own, he might control them for their own good, and other people's too. You know, sir, a wrecker needn't be a thief. When things are washed on shore, or when our men, at the risk of their lives

fish them out of the ocean, and when there
is no owner to claim them, I think we have
a better right to them than anybody else.
Then, what a chance we have here, for showing humanity to ship-wrecked people!
There's no telling, sir, how many of them
poor unfortunates you might save from
perishing in the course of a year, and what
a reform you might make among the wreckers themselves."

Ferrand was silent for some moments,
while he considered the subject in this new
light. Amidst the agitation and hurry of
his thoughts, just then, the idea of asking
God to guide him aright, never occurred to
his mind. He was what we may term a
half-religious man, and the sort of instinctive
respect which he felt for holy things was
owing to the teachings of a Christian mother,
whose gentle guidance he had lost when

about sixteen years old. His father was spared for several years later, but his care was almost entirely centered on the cultivation of his son's mind, as Francis was really a youth of very promising talents, and, had he not been born rich, might have "made his mark" in the world. But, being trained to no particular occupation, the energy of his nature was never fully developed, and he acquired a thoughtlessness of character that clung to him through life. His aim was to enjoy the present hour as fully as possible, in a refined and graceful sort of way, and without wronging anybody else.

The lovely and pious young lady whom he married had,—more by her example than by anything she said,—"almost persuaded" him "to be a Christian;" but the difficulty was that he could not come up to the reality of believing himself to be a great sinner. "I have never done much harm," he would say, "and I never meant to do any." He persuaded himself that with just a little religion to piece out his own merits, he might easily manage to get to Heaven. He went to church quite frequently, and on Sunday, would pick out and read some of the most interesting narratives, and poetic portions of the Bible.

Now, while Lieutenant Ferrand was considering the arguments that Giles had urged, his whole frame became agitated with perplexity. He cast alternate glances at Giles, at the floor, and at the windows, as if in hopes of seeing something that might help him in making up his mind;—but, as we said before, he somehow forgot to look to God.

"Why," said he, at length, though in a hesitating tone,—"if I can do any good by spending a year among these people,—that must, certainly, make a difference. I think I will try the experiment."

As he spoke, however, the blood again tingled in his cheeks, and he pressed one hand over his eyes, in an agony of shame at having accepted Giles's offer, under any pretence. The old sailor perceived this spasm, and said hastily, "Well, sir, I pledge you my word that I will do all I can to help you in your plans, and try to bring about a better state of things here. But be so kind, now, as to come with me to my cabin, and get a cup of coffee, and a little breakfast."

Lieutenant Ferrand promptly rose, gave himself a slight shake, and put on his hat. He did not care anything about breakfast, just then, but he felt eager for some change of scene and of subject.

When the Lieutenant and Giles emerged

from the hut, most of the wreckers were standing in a group, a little distance off, talking together. Ferrand wore a neat undress uniform, and a very becoming straw hat, and there was something in his whole appearance which might have riveted the attention, and struck the fancy of wiser people than the Florida wreckers.

"Well, boys,"—exclaimed Giles, as he pointed to the Lieutenant, "here is our new Commodore."

All the wreckers immediately pulled off their hats, tossed them up in the air, and gave three vehement hurrahs, while Lieutenant Ferrand bowed slightly in return, and forced himself to smile. The wreckers then crowded around him to shake hands, and to show their cordiality of feeling, they thought themselves bound to shake his hand as violently as possible. Ferrand soon showed by his looks that he was tired of this kind of exercise, and Giles persuaded the other wreckers to put off the rest of the hand-shaking until some future time, and allow the Lieutenant, just now, to take a cup of coffee.

After taking a little refreshment, Lieutenant Ferrand's next act was to sit down and write a letter to his wife. He briefly informed her that his West India speculation had failed, and that his yacht had run ashore on the Florida coast, and was considerably injured, but that he had unexpectedly received "an appointment," which he ingeniously, but not very clearly described as that of being "a sort of wreck-master," for this portion of the coast. He stated that the duties of this office might keep him absent from home for a year, but that his salary would enable him to send his wife enough money to support her and their little one in

comfort, for that period of time, at least. In
conclusion, he promised Blanche that she
should receive letters from him very frequently, and gave such directions as would
enable her messages to reach him, in return.

Ferrand's chest, and all its contents, had
now been given back to him, and he enclosed
in this letter to his wife several bank-notes,
which comprised very nearly all the money
he had. When the letter was ready, Giles
undertook to see that it was put in the way
of safely reaching its destination.

On the afternoon of the next day, Hugh
was wandering listlessly along the beach,
while the wrecker's children played noisily
and boisterously about, and some of the boys
every now and then disturbed Hugh's meditations, by calling to him to " come and have
some fun," or by playing him some mischiev-
ous trick, as a penalty for being " so dull and

10

sober." But it was now young Ross's particular wish to be left to himself, and as, in looking across the intervening water, he saw the quiet beauty of Von Ulden's island, it struck him that there would be a good place in which to seek for peace and solitude. Accordingly, he jumped into a little boat, took the oars, and rowed himself to the island. There he sat himself down, near the shore, upon the roots of an old tree, which had been laid bare by the washing of the waves at high tide. Hugh rested his elbows on his knees, his chin upon his hands, looking straight before him. His expression of face grew more and more sad, and he had just heaved a sigh so deep that it was almost a groan, when a slight rustling near by attracted his attention, and caused him to look around. Hugh's ideas concerning angels were the most crude and dim imaginable, and referred only to wings and long white robes; but we cannot blame him for this, since it was only recently that by reading Lieutenant Ferrand's books, he had learned that such beings exist at all. But the book which Hugh had read most attentively was "The Arabian Nights," and from its pages he had gathered pretty distinct notions of what fairies were supposed to be;—nor had he the slightest doubt of the reality of those charming and highly gifted beings.

Therefore, after staring for a moment or two at the girl who stood not far from him, Hugh seriously and deferentially inquired. "Are you a fairy, Miss?"

Now, the few books which Marianna had read, all happened to be true ones, and, in the knowledge of fictitious things, even Hugh was in advance of her.

"A fairy!"—she repeated, with surprise,

"what is that?— I am Marianna Von Ulden, and my grandfather's house is over there, among the orange trees."

"Well," returned the boy, "I am Hugh Ross;—but I wish that I was almost anybody else."

"Why?" asked Marianna.

"Because," said Hugh, anxious to unburden his heart to a listener of such amiable appearance,—"because there's nobody in this whole world that cares one straw about me, or wants me to care anything about them. My father was buried this morning,—but he never thought me of any account when he was living. I had one friend that did a great deal for me, and that I would be willing to die for this minute,—and that's Lieutenant Ferrand. But as my horrid bad luck would have it,—he must be the very one to shoot my father;—and *now*, I can see that he don't care about having me near him. It seems as if he blames me for still liking him, after what has happened.

"Old Giles has given me a home, just so that Lieutenant Ferrand may have me to wait on him, and still, I don't wait on him much, because he won't give me a chance to. I don't know what's to become of me, or what kind of a man I'm to grow up to be.—I've got nothing to do, nothing to learn, nobody to talk to, and no one to care whether I live or die!"

Hugh's words, and the melancholy, hopeless way in which they were spoken, easily drew forth the sympathy of Marianna.

"Well," said she, "the time was when I had a good many that loved me, and that I love still, though they are gone from me now. I can just faintly remember my mother,—like a dream of an angel,—and how

10*

she held me to her bosom and kissed me.
My father, too, was very fond of me, I know;
and then I had aunt Naomi,—such a good
kind nurse,—Oh, there never was another
like her! Now, I have no one but grandfather, and *he* has so much to worry him.—
But what am I talking about!—I have some
one else, to be sure, who loves me better
than even a mother, or a father, could. As
aunt Naomi's hymn-book says,

> "One there is above all others,
>   Well deserves the name of friend."

"That Friend watches over me by night
and by day,—saves me from danger, even
before I know that any danger is near;—
cheers my heart when I am sad,—tells me
when I do wrong, and helps me do right.
I'm perfectly sure that Friend will never for-
sake me, and will never feel displeased with
me, unless it's for some good cause."

"I wish that I had such a friend as that," said Hugh with a sigh."

"Why, you can have," answered Marianna; "He is willing to be the friend of anybody that will ask him.

Then seeing that Hugh looked surprised and perplexed, she inquired, "Don't you know anything about Jesus, the Saviour?"

"Yes;"—said Hugh, "the sailor boy that taught me how to read had no book except a Bible that his parents had given him, and so I learned out of that. The last part of it was about Jesus,—how he cured sick people, and gave sight to the blind,—and many other things that I don't remember. But how can he care anything about us? He is in Heaven now,—and we are way down here, upon this earth!"

"Why," said Marianna, very earnestly, "He is the same with God, the Maker of this island, that main-land, that great ocean, and everything else that's in this world;—and don't you think that he who made everything can see and know everything? He is looking at you and me standing here, at this moment;—He listens to our words, and reads every thought in our hearts. Yes,—though we can't see him, He is right *here* now; to his believing disciples his promise is, "I am with you always."

As Marianna emphatically pronounced this great truth, a sudden conviction of its reality darted through Hugh's whole being, like an electric thrill. Starting to his feet, he looked around him. A mysterious brightness seemed to rest upon that blooming isle,—that snowy beach, and wide-spread ocean,—because Christ was there! With feelings somewhat like those of Paul, when that wondrous light broke upon his vision, near Damascus, Hugh said, half to himself and half to Marianna, " But how can I tell what Jesus wants me to do ?"

" Have you no Bible," asked Marianna.

" No indeed;—I never had one," answered Hugh.

Marianna reflected a few moments, then said, "Well, I will give you aunt Naomi's Bible. I don't know that I ever could give it away, if she hadn't said to me, just a few days before she died, " Dear child, when I am gone, and you meet with some poor soul that has no Bible, give him this." I told her that I should never like to part with it, but she said, " Yes,—Bibles are to do good with, and not to keep hoarded up. You have one that your dear mother left, and you must keep it always." So, wait here Hugh, and I will soon be back."

Marianna tripped away to her grandfather's

house, and speedily returned with the Bible.
She could not refrain from a sigh, and a
moistening of the eyes, as she placed in
Hugh's hands that volume which she had
seen her dear nurse read so often, but she
comforted herself by saying to the boy, " I'm
sure that if reading this makes you better,
and happier, I shall only be carrying out
aunt Naomi's last wish in giving it to you."

As soon as he received the Bible, Hugh
opened it, turned over a leaf or two, and
glanced anxiously at the pages.

" When I read a book," said he, " I always
like to understand it, and I don't know as I
can understand everything in this."

" Then you must ask God to help you understand it," replied Marianna.

As Hugh had never tried to pray, he felt
doubtful whether he could proceed rightly
in offering a petition to the Sovereign of the

universe. Marianna saw this in his looks,
and thus continued; "You must just go
where you can be quiet by yourself, and
kneel down, and raise your thoughts to God,
and ask Him, for Jesus' sake, to teach you
the right meaning of what you read in His
holy book. Remember, He can hear you as
well from the Florida beach, as if you were
kneeling right before His throne in heaven!"

Again Hugh involuntarily glanced around
and upward, and, awe-struck in the felt presence of "the King eternal, immortal and
invisible,—" he reverently replied, "I'll do
as you say."

"Yes, and I, too, will pray for you," said
Marianna. "But good-bye, Hugh;—it is time
for me to be going home."

Hugh thanked Marianna, with unfeigned
warmth, for her precious gift, and stood looking after her until she had flitted out of

sight. Then, putting the Bible in his bosom, he jumped into his boat, and returned to the main-land. He inquired if Lieutenant Ferrand had anything for him to do, and, on being answered in the negative, he at once went to the garret room where he slept under the sloping and moss-covered roof of Giles's cottage. Hugh very sensibly began by kneeling down and uttering a short prayer for Divine help to understand what he should read. He then opened his Bible at the New Testament, and was soon absorbed in studying the teachings, the sufferings, and the redeeming love of Jesus.

CHAPTER VII.

LIEUTENANT FERRAND DISCOVERS HIS MISTAKE. HE VISITS VON ULDEN'S ISLAND.—HUGH LEAVES THE WRECKER SETTLEMENT.

THE next day Lieutenant Ferrand, for the first time, stepped upon the strand of Von Ulden's island. His motives in coming were similar to those which had led Hugh thither the preceding afternoon. His mind was dissatisfied;—he was restless;—and the quiet, retired appearance of this island seemed to promise a pleasing means of escape from disagreeable company. On the first evening after accepting the office of "Commander," Lieutenant Ferrand began to realize how difficult was the task he had undertaken—to reform the wreckers. That evening, they held a festive meeting in hon-

11

or of their "New Commodore," and Lieutenant Ferrand was obliged to take the head
of the table, and preside over a scene which
he heartily detested. He firmly declined to
do more than taste the liquor which was
placed before him, although repeatedly urged
to drink; and he patiently endured the
clouds of tobacco smoke, and the almost constant spitting of the tobacco chewers,—though
he never used the noxious weed in any form.

But scarcely could he hide the disgust pro-
duced by the shocking profanity of those
around him. His mother had impressed upon his mind such an abhorrence of this habit
that it could never be effaced, and the first
piece of advice he had given Hugh Ross was
an injunction to leave off swearing,—which
Hugh did from that hour.

The wreckers soon became drunk and
noisy, and the room where they were assem-

bled resounded with roaring laughter and vulgar songs. When he had endured his penance as long as possible, Ferrand rose, bade the company good night, and left the apartment.

The wreckers thought this singular behaviour, and yet they felt it as a relief, for Lieutenant Ferrand's presence was a restraint upon them, and they had been obliged to make some effort to "enjoy themselves" while he saw and heard them.

The next day, Ferrand commenced a practice which afterwards became habitual with him,—that of roaming about through the vicinity, "killing time," and trying to kill thought, by viewing the charms of natural scenery in a part of the world which he had never visited before. On the third morning, his restless mood led him, as we have said, to Von Ulden's island. Hugh managed the oars of the little boat which performed this short voyage, and when Lieutenant Ferrand stepped on shore, Hugh made fast the boat and followed him. Ferrand walked leisurely along, looking at the island scenery, and on catching sight of Von Ulden's house, turned his steps in that direction.

He had almost reached the dwelling when, coming along a foot-path through the luxuriant grass, there appeared Von Ulden, leaning upon the shoulder of Marianna. This meeting was accidental, and when Marianna saw the Lieutenant, she tried to turn her grandfather's steps in another direction, but it was too late. Von Ulden immediately judged who Lieutenant Ferrand was, and Ferrand, on his part, made an equally successful guess, from seeing the old man supported by Marianna. A boding scowl came over Von Ulden's face as he saw the Lieu-

tenant, but Ferrand looked tranquil and unconscious, as he picked his teeth with the
point of a bird's quill, which he had found
a few minutes before.

"You are the new Commodore, I suppose?" said Von Ulden, with a grim sneer,
"I wish you joy of your new dignity!"

Ferrand well understood his meaning, but
he answered gravely, and with a polite in-
clination of the head, "I thank you, sir."
Von Ulden however, seemed to be determined that they should not part upon peace-
able terms, and he remarked with the same
air of savage derision, "It's laughable to see
full grown ruffians so pleased with a new
toy, that, after awhile, will be broken and
thrown aside! You may thank your stars,
my little gentleman, that old Von Ulden's
word is not as powerful as it once was, or

11*

you would have been hung up two or three
days ago!"

"I know it," answered Lieutenant Ferrand,
composedly, "and, though I have a great
aversion to hanging, I begin to think that, if
you could have persuaded them to kill me
in any other way, it would have been a very
friendly act."

"You mock me, do you, puppy ;—you pre-
tend to think the old broken down wrecker
not worth quarrelling with," exclaimed Von
Ulden, rapidly working himself into a passion. "What brings you here, to beard me
at my own door? You shall find it a dear
experiment !—You shall learn what it is to
come and defy the tiger in his lair !"

As he thus spoke, Von Ulden drew forth
a long bladed, sharp pointed knife, which he
always carried, and, pushing aside Marianna,
advanced toward the Lieutenant.

Ferrand stirred not a step to avoid the knife, but drawing his coat away from the left side of his bosom, touched his vest right over the heart, and said, "Strike me here, and strike hard!"

The two children, who had been astonished spectators of this scene, saw that Von Ulden was actually about to take his life, without fear or hesitation, and they both sprang forward. Marianna caught hold of her grand-father's arm, and Hugh wrested away the knife, which he then flung into a thicket at some distance. Highly indignant, young Ross exclaimed, "Old man, if it was not for *her*," pointing to Marianna, "I would soon tell you what I think of you!"

"Hush;" said Lieutenant Ferrand,—" you had better think if you and I may not come to be as wicked as he is, by the time our hair is as white!"

Hugh looked at the aged sinner before him,
—recalled the conversation he had held with
Marianna the preceding day, and the good
resolutions which he had formed that morning, over the open pages of his newly acquired Bible,—and he wondered, with a
shudder, if all those resolutions could fail,
and he be left, at length, to such an old age
as this!

Again, as on a former occasion which we
have described, there came over Von Ulden's
face a sudden change, from rage to anguish
and despair. "Yes," he groaned, "I am fit
for nothing now! Even children can baffle
me;—and I have lost the power to revenge
myself on any one!"

With these words, he staggered to a fallen
tree near by, sat down upon it, and dropping
his head forward and shutting his eyes,

seemed to sink into a partially insensible condition.

" Ah," said Marianna, with pallid cheeks and quivering lip, addressing herself to the Lieutenant and Hugh, " if you knew how much grandfather suffers, you would pity and not hate him !"

" I do pity him, my dear," said Lieutenant Ferrand.

" I believe you do, sir," replied Marianna, looking at him gratefully, " but I must say that you are a great deal too careless of your own life."

" I don't know," answered Ferrand, " I felt just now as if I might as well meet death at once, before I found any more troubles ; and I should never have had that trial to go through with again, since ' It is appointed unto men but once to die.' "

" But, after that, *the judgment*," impressively and significantly added Marianna, finishing the quotation.

Ferrand cast down his eyes, and Marianna saw that he, who had so calmly braved death a few minutes before, shrank from the thought of that decision which might be passed upon his soul by the Almighty Judge, should he now be hurried into eternity.

He said nothing, however, but, after standing in pensive meditation for a few minutes, bowed to Marianna and walked away, followed by Hugh.

The wreckers were now, by Lieutenant Ferrand's directions, engaged in repairing the yacht, and making it seaworthy, so that it might be used by them as a trading vessel to carry to neighboring ports such goods as they wished to dispose of.

This did much towards rendering their new leader popular with the wreckers. Indeed, his influence over them was wonderful, considering that he never joined in their drinking parties, and rarely held a conversation with any of them except Giles and his wife, with whom he resided. But the fact that there was a great deal in his behaviour which they could not understand, gave the wreckers a much higher opinion of Lieutenant Ferrand; as people are more apt to respect that which is mysterious, and above their comprehension. Besides, Ferrand had a very amiable disposition;—a gift which renders goodness ten times more attractive, and makes even the erring and benighted soul seem not less than an "angel ruined." The blending of mildness and dignity in the Lieutenant's actions and language, made a still deeper impression on those around him, because they had been accustomed to the harshness and violence of Von Ulden, and

they found that their new Commodore
could be just as firm and decided as the old
one, without being unreasonable or passion-
ate.

Ferrand was much more pleased to converse with the women and children of the
wrecker families than with the men; and his
manner towards these two classes was full of
that noble gentleness which some people call
"chivalry," but which is nothing more than
doing to others as we would have them do to
us, if we were weak and timid, and they
were brave and strong.

About ten days had elapsed since Lieutenant Ferrand's first arrival in Florida, when
a violent gale sprang up, which caused a
small merchant vessel to be wrecked upon
that portion of the coast. The wreckers, as
usual, thought of nothing but securing whatever articles of value were to be picked up,

and the master of the vessel and three men who were with him, might have perished in the waves, if Lieutenant Ferrand, with Giles and Hugh, had not gone to their relief in a small boat, and rescued them, at the peril of their own lives. When the four sea-faring men found all their property in the hands of the wreckers, they remonstrated against such conduct, but nothing was given them except a dry suit of clothes for each one, and they were soon made to understand that their lives would be in danger if they said anything more. The master of the vessel was in despair at his loss, and exclaimed to Lieutenant Ferrand, "If I'd known that your men were going to plunder me of everything, in this way, I'd as lief have been drowned!"

Ferrand was vexed and mortified beyond expression, and knowing that it would be useless to command the wreckers to give up

12

their plunder to its proper owner, he tried to persuade them into doing so, by talking to them as though they were persons of honorable and benevolent feelings. But these lawless men considered his remonstrances only as a proof of what they termed "greenness," and positively, yet respectfully, declared that "such a thing as *that* would never do!"

"Findings is keepings;—that's wrecker's law, sir," added one of them, triumphantly.

Ferrand walked away in disgust, feeling that all the hold which he had upon these men was surely not enough to produce any great reformation among them. It is true that missionaries in foreign lands, behold the most ferocious and degraded savages transformed into good and useful men; but these missionaries have a secret of power which Ferrand did not possess. Before there can be any great change in a person's life, the heart must be changed, and nothing can change the heart but the power of the Holy Spirit. Ferrand had not learned by his own experience the wonder-working power of Gospel faith, and when mere morality,—which he expected would have the effect of a wizard's wand,—proved to be a dead and brittle stick in his grasp,—he felt completely helpless and baffled.

The wreckers now set about dividing their spoils, and Lieutenant Ferrand was summoned to preside, and see that it was done fairly. He promptly complied with this request, and nothing but his deep seriousness, and the fewness of his words, showed that he remembered the difference of opinion between himself and his followers.

A choice and liberal share was, by the general vote, alloted to their new "Commodore,"

and he immediately had the articles conveyed
to a spot not far off, where he had directed
the ship-wrecked sailors to wait until they
should hear from him. Giles's conscience
had taken a fresh alarm from some words
that had been addressed to him by Lieutenant Ferrand, and he immediately consented
to give up to the ship-wrecked men his share
also of their cargo and personal property.
The sailors purchased for a trifle, from one of
the wreckers, a four-oared boat in which they
placed the goods that had been returned to
them, and started off to seek along the coast,
for some more hospitable place of rest.

Lieutenant Ferrand's heart now felt wonderfully light. It was very cheering to think
that after all, he could do some good by re-
maining, for a time, among the wreckers, and
restoring to ship-wrecked people as much of

their property as fell to the shares of himself and Giles.

It was not until an hour afterwards that
the idea struck him,—"But how, then, can
I do anything for my family, if, by remain-
ing here, I gain nothing but my own subsis-
tence?"

The more he thought of this difficulty, the
worse it appeared. He felt like a bird en-
tangled in a net, vainly beating its wings in
the effort to fly, but becoming every moment
more involved in the cunning snare. While
Ferrand was pacing up and down his room,
trying to decide what course he should pursue, there was a rap at the door, and, on the
Lieutenant's saying, "come in," Giles made
his appearance.

"The gale is blowing up hard again, sir,"
said he, "and there's a vessel going to pieces
off the south-west."

12*

"We must try and save the men on board," said Lieutenant Ferrand, eagerly.

"Oh, that ain't possible, sir!" answered Giles. "She's too far off, and the sea's too rough for a small boat ever to get near her."

On looking out upon the ocean, Lieutenant Ferrand saw that this was indeed true, and even while he looked, the ill-fated vessel disappeared entirely, beneath the furiously tossing waves.

As soon as the gale had abated, the wreckers were out in their boats, picking up whatever articles from the wreck drifted along upon the water, and bringing up some others by fishing for them with their grappling irons.

Having no better occupation at present, Lieutenant Ferrand also went out in a boat with Giles and Hugh, and assisted in gathering in the wrecker's harvest. On returning to the shore again, he found upon the beach the bodies of two drowned men, one of whom was the commander of the sunken vessel. Some of the wreckers had already commenced to plunder these bodies, and, after taking from them everything of value, gave them a rude and hasty burial.

Lieutenant Ferrand knew that, by the letters and other papers found upon the drowned men,—by marks upon their clothing, or similar means,—he could probably find out who they were, and where their families resided; and conscience said, to those families belonged everything of value that had been the property of the dead. But he stifled these thoughts, and said to himself, "I cannot help it. I *must* have something to send to Blanche."

The next morning, Lieutenant Ferrand's yacht, under the command of Giles, sailed to a neighboring sea-port, to dispose of goods which had been obtained from the recent wrecks. Giles himself was too ignorant a man, and had been too long a wrecker, to perceive that he was doing anything amiss in appropriating the property of the drowned sailors, and his wife gravely remarked, " I'm sure it's well for us, and for them poor souls, too, that they've all gone to a better world; —for, this plan of the Lieutenant's, about keeping nothing for yourself if there's anybody else to claim it, may all sound very good; but you and I, Giles, can't live on nothing, and we're too old to go to work!"

In a few days the yacht returned, and the money for which the cargo had been sold was divided among the wreckers.

They allotted a liberal share to Lieutenant Ferrand, and he immediately dispatched it in a letter to his wife.

After seeing the letter duly started upon its journey, he returned to his own apartment, locked the door, and, throwing himself upon his bed, buried his face in the pillow, as though he felt himself unworthy to behold the light of day.

"Now," he ejaculated, "I have, indeed, fallen! Francis Ferrand, whose name was never mentioned in the same breath with meanness or dishonor, has shared with villains their plunder, and kept what rightfully belonged to the widow and orphan!"

This thought made the unhappy man writhe as if, like the Mexican Emperor of old, he had been stretched upon a bed of burning coals, and not upon the couch where only the night before, he had enjoyed a sound and refreshing sleep. In a little while, he became more calm, (though not more contented,) and then he asked himself, "But, how did I ever come to this?"

His thoughts ran back over all his preceding life, even to the period of early childhood. He saw himself again fondled in the arms of that sweet mother whose only fault was that she could see nothing in her darling child but what was lovable. Again he heard his father telling over, with proud satisfaction, all his hopes of what their noble boy would prove to be, in the future. And how much Frank had been loved and petted by all around him, whether relations, neighbors, acquaintances or servants! He was so pretty, so intelligent, so good-humored and affectionate! And, in addition to all these pleasing gifts of nature, he was the only child of wealthy parents,—the heir of luxury and splendor.

To such a one, the Saviour had said, of

old, "*one thing* thou lackest;"—and this was
Ferrand's case, but yet he knew it not.

While thinking over all the happy past,—
that had now vanished as completely as last
night's dream,—Lieutenant Ferrand was a-
roused by a slight tapping at his room-door.
He rose from the bed, smoothed back his
disordered hair, drank a glass of water, and
then, with seeming composure, unlocked and
opened the door. Hugh stood there, and
said modestly,—"Mrs. Giles says sir, shall
she bring your supper to your room?"

"No, I thank her;" answered the Lieutenant, "I shall not take supper this evening.
Have you had yours yet Hugh?"

"No, sir," replied the boy. "Well," said
Ferrand, "get your supper, and then come
to me again. I want to have a talk with
you."

"Very well, sir;—but I know that Mrs,

Giles would like you to eat something. You
ai'nt sick,—are you, Lieutenant Ferrand?"

"No;—only tired. Go, now;—but don't
forget to come again, after awhile." Hugh,
accordingly, went away to his supper, but
made that meal much shorter than usual,
from a wish to hear as soon as possible, what
it was that Lieutenant Ferrand had to say to
him. On going to his room again, he found
him seated in an old-fashioned, high-backed,
arm-chair, which, as one of the few articles
of luxury that Giles's cottage contained, had
been placed in the honored boarder's apartment. Ferrand commenced the conversation immediately, by saying, Hugh, you are
growing to be a very tall boy. In a few
years, you will be a man.—But, have you any
idea what you intend to be, when you grow
up?"

"No, sir," answered Hugh, earnestly,

" I've thought of it, many a time ;—but still
I feel just like somebody that's walking ·
through a thick fog, and can't see two steps
before him !"

"That is pretty much the case with me,"
said Ferrand with an involuntary sigh. " But
you wouldn't wish to be a *wrecker*, like these
men around us ?"

Hugh did not answer immediately, for this
question had, of late, been puzzling him a great
deal. Ever since he first knew Lieutenant
Ferrand, he had regarded him as a faultless
model of conduct, and as one who had at-
tained the highest perfection that human
nature can reach. When his " bright particular star" became the leader of the wreckers, Hugh did not presume to doubt that
now, as ever, the Lieutenant was doing the
best thing possible. But, since Marianna
had given him aunt Naomi's Bible, Hugh

13

had been studying it diligently, and, several
times had visited the island, to obtain Marianna's assistance in finding out the meaning
of passages which perplexed him. He soon
perceived that from the eighth command-
ment in the Old Testament to the Golden
Rule in the New, the wreckers were breaking all the laws of God, and he began to feel
like Bunyan's Pilgrim when he first discovered that his dwelling was in the city of
Destruction. Yet how was he to reconcile
the teachings of the Bible, in this respect,
with his rooted opinion of Lieutenant Ferrand's infallibility ? It was no wonder that,
when the Lieutenant himself called upon
him to settle this delicate question, poor
Hugh at first, was silent and confused, and
that his face turned a very deep scarlet.

"Tell me," repeated Lieutenant Ferrand,

"do you wish to grow up to be a wrecker, like those around us?"

"Why, sir, what else can I be, if I stay here," said Hugh. "And I'm sure I want to stay here as long as you do."

"But you shall not," emphatically rejoined Ferrand. "If you stay here, you will come to be a lawless ruffian, with very little more sense or feeling than the rocks in yonder reef. I find that I myself have committed a great mistake by consenting to become mixed up with these wreckers;—but if I can help it, you shall not be ruined by my folly."

"But what would you want me to do, sir?" asked Hugh.

"I will send you," answered Ferrand, "to your mother's relations, in Tallahassee, and they must put you in the way of learning to make a decent and honest living."

"Oh, Lieutenant Ferrand," ejaculated

Hugh, with a full heart,—"we have been together so long—in good days and in bad!"

"I know it," said Lieutenant Ferrand,
"and I have ever found you a good and faithful boy. But now to see you staying for
my sake, among these wreckers, growing into
their ways, and learning nothing that is good,
would only make me more unhappy than I
am. If you wish to comfort me, or give me
pleasure, leave this nest of thieves, and let
me hear that you are making for yourself a
place among respected and honorable men.
Will you do this?"

" Yes sir ;—I will," answered Hugh, with
a powerful effort.

" That is right," said Ferrand. " Go, now,
bundle up your clothes, and be ready to leave
this place early to-morrow morning. But
just before you start, let me have another
word with you."

Hugh bent his head, in silence, and left the presence of Lieutenant Ferrand.

The next morning he stood before the Lieutenant again, dressed for his journey, and with a bundle of clothing in his hand. Ferrand gave him some directions as to the route which he should travel. He then put into young Ross's hand a few gold pieces, which were all the money he possessed, though he did not inform Hugh of this fact.

"Now," said he, "only be steady and industrious, and you may hope for a contented and comfortable life,—perhaps a great and noble one. Don't be sorry that you are beginning the world as a poor boy, with nothing but God and your own hands to depend upon! Be thankful that you have no chance to waste all the spring of your life, as I have done, in idleness, and amusement, and to find

13*

yourself at three and thirty, without any particular way of earning your support, and with habits that unfit you for plain and honest labor! No, Hugh;—I hope that you will be able to give in a better account.— Good-bye."

He extended his hand. Hugh clasped it in both his own, and for two or three minutes pressed it tightly against his heart. He then released that hand, which had never touched him except in kindness, and murmuring, "Good-bye sir," moved toward the door. Suddenly he stopped; leaned against the wall and placed one arm across his face. Those were no idle, boyish tears!

Hugh felt that he was now, in all likelihood, parting forever from that friend whom he had so admired, reverenced, and loved.

He knew that his departure would leave Lieutenant Ferrand in the midst of that

rude and uncongenial band of wreckers,
without a single face to look upon that had
become familiar to him in happier days. It
was but a few moments that Hugh gave way
entirely, and then he fairly ran from the
room, and out of the house.

CHAPTER VIII.

HUGH DISAPPEARS, FOR THE PRESENT.—TER-
RIBLE STORM AND WRECK OF A STEAM-
SHIP.—LIEUTENANT FERRAND AND
MARIANNA FIND GREAT TREAS-
URES IN THE OCEAN.

BY Lieutenant Ferrand's directions, Giles was waiting in a small boat, to convey Hugh for some distance along the coast.

As the boat put off, Hugh looked towards Von Ulden's island, and saw Marianna standing upon the shore. He had no chance to bid her adieu in words, but he took off his hat, waved it towards her, and then drew from his bundle, and held up in her sight, the Bible which she had given him.

Marianna waved her hand in return,—understanding that Hugh was going away, though she imagined that he would not be absent long.

Towards sunset, the next day, Marianna crossed over to the main-land, in order to purchase some tobacco for her grandfather's smoking, which was his chief means of passing away time. After she had procured the tobacco, the wrecker's wife from whom she bought it, insisted upon her eating some fine strawberries, which she set before her. Then, as it was fast growing dark, Marianna started off towards the little boat which had brought her from the island. But the sky had now become overspread with huge black clouds, and a breeze was blowing which caused every tree-leaf and grass-blade to tremble and shudder, as if in dread of the coming storm. Just as Marianna came to the beach, a loud

peal of thunder was heard, and the red lightning, with its zig-zag line, shot through the
sable clouds like a swift-falling stream of
liquid fire.

"Oh, Peter," exclaimed Marianna to the
colored boy, who was just about getting into
the boat, "do you think we can reach the
island before the storm comes on?"

Peter shook his head with a grave and
doubtful look, but accomodatingly replied,
"Don't know, Miss;—just as you say."

"No;—you are in my dominions, now,
and I have something to say about it," smil-
ingly remarked Lieutenant Ferrand, who had
come up unobserved. "Get out of that
boat, Peter, and draw it up on shore. Miss
Marianna will not attempt to go across until
the storm is over."

"But," said Marianna, "I am afraid that
my grandfather will be uneasy about me, if

I don't come home soon. He might think that I had tried to cross, and that something had happened to the boat."

" He would think so, and then find out that he had made only too true a guess, if you did attempt to cross," rejoined Lieutenant Ferrand.

At this moment, Marianna saw the widow woman who did the heaviest house-work of Von Ulden's family, come down to the island shore. She saw upon the opposite beach the person for whom she was looking, and screamed out, at the top of her voice, " Miss Marianna, don't try to come over until the storm's done!"

" No, she will not," called out Lieutenant Ferrand, in reply.

Just then, there arose such a wind as immediately took off Peter's hat and carried it out to sea, and which would have made Marianna and the Lieutenant undergo similar losses, if they had not seized hold of their hats at the critical moment. The widow ran back to Von Ulden's house as fast as she could, and Mrs Giles, coming to the door of the cottage, cried out, "Come in here, Miss Marianna, quick!—Lieutenant, hadn't you better come in?"

Marianna at once accepted the invitation, and took the chair which Old Giles placed for her in the sitting room of the cottage. Mrs. Giles sat down near her, and knitted at a blue yarn stocking while she talked about the weather, and other such common-place subjects. Lieutenant Ferrand, when he came in, placed himself by one of the windows, and looked out upon the gathering storm. Night seemed to come more quickly than usual, and it was a night without a ray from moon or star. Can-

14

dles were lighted in Giles's dwelling and the other cottages, and the wreckers looked forth eagerly, in the hope that some sad misfortune to their fellow beings might bring a little worldly profit to them. There were frequent peals of thunder, and vivid flashes of lightning, that gave a red tinge to the dusky waves of the troubled ocean, and showed their white crests of boiling foam. But now, when the thunder's voice was silent for a little while, another booming sound was heard. The wreckers quickly recognized the minute guns of some vessel in distress. At the next lightning flash, all eyes eagerly scanned the ocean, and a steam vessel was seen, driven along towards the coast by the furious power of wind and wave. The huge surges that dashed over her decks, and the violence with which she was pitched from side to side, showed how terrifying and full of confusion must be the situation of those on board.

Two of the wreckers entered Giles's cottage, and one of them, in a jovial mood, said to Lieutenant Ferrand, "Eh, Commodore, I guess there'll soon be some pickings off that big vessel!"

Ferrand made no reply, but looked at him with contempt, and then, starting up, went forth into the dark and stormy night, The steamer had been driven nearer to the coast, and suddenly a loud crash was heard, amidst the noise of the winds and waters. At the same instant, there went up a shriek of agony from hundreds of human voices, and words of earnest supplication to God were wrung from the hearts of many who, when they were safe at home, had mocked at the thought of prayer.

All of the wreckers hurried to the beach,

and many of their wives went with them, no
less fearless than their husbands, and no less
eager in their desire for plunder.

Others like Marianna and Mrs. Giles, remained in their cottages, but pressed their
faces against the window-panes, in an endeavor to see out upon the darkened ocean.
Presently, another lightning flash displayed
to all eyes a fearful sight. The foundering
steamer lay helplessly upon the rocks, and
her deck was covered with men, women, and
children, calling wildly for help. Again the
black darkness wrapped them all up, and
oh, how deep a gloom was that, to those poor
ship-wrecked sufferers! Marianna, pale,
trembling, and heart-sick, wrung her hands
in an agony of sympathy, and then clasped
them tightly together, as she leaned against
the frame of the window by which she stood.

"Oh," said she to herself, "if the poor

people on board that ship would only think of doing as aunt Naomi told me to do, when grandfather's vessel was wrecked! They would not feel so much afraid if, instead of looking at the foundering vessel, or the terrible sea, they looked right up to God!"

Marianna resolved that she herself would do this, and turning her gaze away from the window, she poured out her soul in supplication to God for those who were in such fearful peril.

Just then, another lightning flash showed to Ferrand, and the other lookers on, that the steamer was rapidly going to pieces, and not only fragments of wreck were tossing on the waves, but also the struggling bodies of a number of human beings, who had been washed off the deck.

Ferrand had been silent all along, for he knew, that, without "life-boats," it would be

14*

impossible to reach the steamer. But, at the sight of those drowning victims, he could no longer control himself.

"What are you going to do, sir?" exclaimed the old sailor. "How will drowning yourself help them?"

Ferrand was silent for a moment, and then ordered the wreckers who were nearest to him to bring two large coils of rope.

. At his command, two men took hold of one end of a rope, while the other end was flung out upon the sea, towards the nearest of those who were struggling in the waves.

The other rope was managed by Lieutenant Ferrand and Giles, but the first, second, and third efforts that were made to throw the lines within reach of any of the sufferers proved unsuccessful. Then, a man succeeded in catching one of the ropes, and was drawn on shore alive, though greatly exhausted.

THE RESCUE.—Page 163.

A few minutes afterwards, the lightning's glare showed the white-clad figure of a woman, driven along through the water, with a child clasped in her arms. She had on a life-preserver, which prevented her from sinking, but she could not resist the power of the waves, which carried her along, not towards the shore, but parallel with it, at a short distance off. The poor lady was too faint and dizzy to utter any cry, and it was easy to see that the manner in which the water kept dashing over them would soon drown both her and the child.

In a moment, Lieutenant Ferrand tied securely around his own waist one end of the rope which he was helping to hold. Giles and another then grasped the opposite end, and Ferrand plunged into the breakers.

The big waves caught him and swept him wildly along, while he was almost suffocated

by the spray which dashed into his face.
He saw the gleam of white garments through
the darkness, sprang forward and seized
them, and found that he had hold of the
mother and child whom he was so anxious to
save. " Pull me in," he shouted. In a few
moments he was dragged on shore, holding
the insensible woman in a clasp not less resolute and faithful than that with which she
held her little child. Pausing but for a
moment, to recover his breath, Ferrand carried the mother and child together to Giles's
cottage. As their clothing was soaked and
streaming with water, he laid them upon a
wooden settle, until they should be relieved
of their wet garments. There, senseless and
pale, they lay, and the mother's long brown
hair, all loose and drenched, trailed down upon the floor. Before he left her to the kindness of Mrs. Giles, Lieutenant Ferrand cast

one anxious glance at the lady's face, to be certain that life yet remained. In saving her life, he had much over-taxed his bodily strength, though he did not feel it at the time.

And now he made a discovery which, coming immediately after that terrible battle with the waves, completely overpowered him. He suddenly became unconscious, and would have fallen to the floor, if Giles had not caught and supported him. He was carried to his own room, and, as no one suspected the true cause of his fainting, Giles felt afraid that the Lieutenant had received some severe hurt, in being dragged upon the shore.

Mrs. Giles and Marianna were now left alone with the half-drowned lady and child, and in looking at the affecting sight before her, the wrecker's wife became a kind and pitying woman, Never, since aunt Naomi's

death, had Marianna had her inmost heart
so thrilled as it was now. Her hands quivered
with agitation, while she assisted Mrs. Giles
in removing the wet clothing of the sufferers.

As a devout Catholic girl, in similar circumstances, might have invoked her favorite
saints, so Marianna, without knowing that
she spoke aloud, kept uttering such ejacula-
tions as " Dear Jesus, spare them !—Let them
live !—Teach us what to do for them !"

Soon the ship-wrecked lady, dressed in a
coarse, but snow-white night-gown, lay upon
Mrs. Giles's bed, still in an unconscious state.
Her long brown tresses were spread out upon the pillow, on either side of a face whose
features were so delicate, and fair, and pale,
and so full of pure and sweet expression,
that Marianna felt as if she were gazing upon the slumbers of a seraph.   The little girl
had already regained her consciousness,—for

a mother's arms had been some shelter to her, even against the roughness of the waves. She was not quite three years old, and her age and circumstances strongly recalled to Marianna that scene in her own life which, though it had happened so long ago, could never be lost to memory. How could she help thinking of the time when she,—but little older than this child,—had been cast by shipwreck upon the same coast?—The first use which the little girl made of her recovered voice was to call again and again upon her mamma, and beg her to "wake up," and then, finding that no answer was returned, she began to cry piteously. Marianna held the child in her arms, and by her caresses and loving words, succeeded in partly soothing its agitation.

Presently, the mother heaved a faint sigh, unclosed a pair of clear, mild, hazel eyes, and

looked around. Marianna immediately placed the little girl upon the bed, beside her, and
the child full of joy at meeting once more its
mother's tender gaze, twined its arms about
her neck, and kissed her again and again.
Instantly the mother's arms were around
her little girl, a smile of rapture lighted up
her face, her eyes were raised to Heaven,
and her lips moved, though no sound was
heard by mortal ears. But the happiness of
that moment was too great for her weakened
frame; her head fell upon the little child's
shoulder, and she again became insensible.
This time, however, she soon revived again,
and lay gazing at her little girl, and receiving
her caresses, with a smile of tranquil joy,
though two large tears were stealing gently
down her cheeks.

Marianna, in the warmth of her heart, embraced and kissed the unknown lady, and

told her how glad she was to see her so far recovered.

"Thank you, dear sweet girl," was the affectionate reply; "you are as good as you are lovely."

Both the mother and the child, tired out as they were, soon dropped into a sound and refreshing sleep. While she and Marianna were watching them, Mrs. Giles heard some one enter the outer room of the cottage, and, going to see who it was, she met Lieutenant Ferrand.

"Ah, how do you feel, now, sir!" asked Mrs. Giles; "you seemed faintish, a little while ago."

"I am well,"—said he, hastily. "How is my wife?"

"Your wife, sir!"

"Yes!—That lady,— tell me,—how is she?"

15

" Why, the lady and her little girl are both getting along nicely. But, you don't mean to say, Lieutenant, that this is Mrs. Ferrand ?"

" It is, indeed," answered he,—"though little did I dream of its being my own wife and child that I was carrying through the breakers!" He covered his face with his hands for a couple of moments, and then, looking up with sudden animation, exclaimed, " But now I must see them!"

" Well, I wouldn't to-night, Lieutenant, if I were you," said Mrs. Giles. " You know the lady,—Mrs. Ferrand,—is most wore out by what she's gone through with, and she and the little girl have just dropped into a nice, sweet sleep, that'll do them more good than a bushel of medicine."

" I will not wake them," said Ferrand, "only let me see them."

"Very well, sir;—but step easy," said Mrs. Giles, leading the way into the other room.

For several minutes, Ferrand stood gazing upon his wife and child, in motionless silence, while Mrs. Giles, in a whisper told Marianna of the strange discovery that had been made.

"Oh, it is wonderful," whispered Marianna, "but God can do anything."

At length Ferrand roused himself, and noiselessly placing a chair by the bed-side, said in a low tone, to Mrs. Giles, "I will sit and watch by them here to-night."

Mrs. Giles and Marianna accordingly withdrew to their own places of rest for the night. Ferrand sat for hours, gazing with a host of thoughts and emotions, upon his sleeping treasures, and it was not till near morning that, overcome by fatigue, his head sunk down in slumber upon the same pillow where reposed his little girl.

Marianna lay awake for a good while, thinking over the strange events of the night. Already she felt that she should enjoy a good deal of pleasure in the company of Mrs. Ferrand and her little girl, and rejoiced over them as two pure, bright jewels, cast by the waves of ocean upon that wild and almost savage coast.

CHAPTER IX.

AFTER THE STORM.—BLANCHE FERRAND DIS-
COVERS THAT HER HUSBAND IS A WRECK-
ER—PLEASANT CHANGES TAKE PLACE
IN MARIANNA'S HOME.

NEXT morning, the sky was blue and sunny as ever before, and the ocean lay in smooth and bright repose. The trees and grass wore a fresher green after the last night's rain, and on Von Ulden's island, the orange blossoms, and wax-like magnolias, scattered around a richer perfume than usual.

But, on the white sand of the beach opposite that island, lay here and there the bodies of drowned men, women and children. Some had, the day before, been poor and humble, and others rich and proud, but there

15*

were no such distinctions among them now.
The great and only difference was, that some
out of the blackness of that stormy night
had soared up to the eternal noonday of
Heaven, and others, when they sank beneath
the sea, went down into that dark and fearful abyss from which lost souls shall never
rise again. But, without one thought of
the awful lesson before their eyes, the wreckers walked along the beach, and greedily
gathered up what articles of value had been
washed ashore that morning. During almost the whole of the previous night, they
had been busy, by the light of pine torches,
in collecting the spoils of the wreck. Even
the children now ran along the shore, picking up what they could, and laughing and
shouting with more than usual gaiety.

All night, Blanche Ferrand's dreams had
been, that she and her child were once more

re-united with the husband and father;—and when, in the morning, she awoke, and found him indeed watching over them, it was a moment of wild, unutterable joy,—yet mixed with a fear that this too might be only a dream. She did not give one thought to the fact that all her worldly possessions had been on board of the wrecked steamer, and were now, most probably, at the bottom of the sea. Her husband and child were the only earthly objects upon which her heart was set, and they,—thanks to the all-merciful One,—were now safe and well, beside her.

Marianna at the first dawn of morning, had hastened over to the island, to assure her grandfather of her safety, and to be scolded by him for being caught in the storm while on the mainland, though he knew perfectly well that she could not possibly avoid it. After taking breakfast with her grandfather, Marianna cleared off the table, and washed and put away the dishes. She then changed her dress, put on her hat, and promising her grandfather that she would soon return, crossed over to the mainland, to see how Mrs. Ferrand and her little girl were. The gush of happiness which she felt at finding herself, her husband and child once more re-united, seemed to restore almost immediately Blanche's bodily strength, and Marianna found her sitting up in the great, high-backed arm chair in Lieutenant Ferrand's room. She wore a flowing white gown, her hair was neatly braided, and Marianna now, for the first time, had the opportunity of judging how very neat and pleasing was Mrs. Ferrand's appearance.

The granddaughter of Von Ulden immediately hastened up to Blanche, exclaiming, "Dear Mrs. Ferrand, I'm so glad to find that you are not sick, after that terrible last night!"

Blanche cordially returned her kiss and embrace, and said to her husband, who sat beside her, "This is another great pleasure for me, in finding here such a dear girl as Maria."

"Marianna"—gently observed the Lieutenant, by way of correction. "Well," was the smiling reply, "I think I have already learned her nature, if not her name, and a charming nature it is."

After a moment's pause, Mrs. Ferrand's countenance suddenly clouded over, with an expression of sadness, and in a low voice, she said, "Frank, there is one thing that I would wish to know, and yet I am afraid to hear it. Of all the people who woke up, well and cheerful, on board that steamer, yesterday morning, how many are there now living upon earth, besides Bessie and me?"

"Indeed, I do not know, as yet," answered Lieutenant Ferrand, "but we cannot help knowing this, that only a few,—a very few of them can possibly have any more of this world's storms to go through with."

There was a silence for some minutes, and then Lieutenant and Mrs. Ferrand began to converse about the impressive fact that Blanche and her child were among the very few that were rescued, and that the appointed means of their rescue was a husband and a father's arm. Marianna had taken little Bessie upon her lap, and was busied in petting and admiring her. She was a plump and healthy child, and her face had that dimpled roundness which we all like to see in little ones of her age. Her complexion, like her mother's was most delicately fair; but the form of her features, her eyes,—so darkly blue, and fringed with such long jetty lashes, and the blackness of her hair, gave her a strange resemblance to Lieutenant Ferrand. Seeing that the child's hair had been trained to cluster in thick short curls, Marianna employed herself in arranging it so, and then viewed with delight the contrast which those curls afforded to Bessie's pink cheeks, and her brow and neck of purest white. The little one had a very slight idea of the danger in which she and her mother had been, the night before, and she did not see anything strange in her father's being with them again. On the morning just before the shipwreck, her mother had promised her that they should "soon see Papa," and Bessie had full faith in that promise.

As Marianna had told her grandfather that she would soon return, she was obliged, in a

little while, to bid good-bye to Mrs. Ferrand
and Bessie, and go back to the island.

A few moments after she had gone, the
wreckers came crouching into Giles's cottage, bringing with them the things which
they had secured from the wreck, and which
they now wished to have fairly divided
among them.

Mrs. Ferrand was startled to hear through
a thin wooden partition, those loud and
rough voices, uttering oaths,—rude contra-
dictions,—and expressions of unfeeling tri-
umph over the quantity of plunder which
they had gained. "Where's the Commodore?" was frequently asked in boisterous
tones.

"For whom are all those men asking?"
inquired Mrs. Ferrand, looking with wonder, at her husband.

"For me," answered Ferrand, forcing a

smile, but at the same time feeling his face suffused with that painful blush which comes when, before those whom we most respect and love, we are compelled to own that the low and degraded are our companions.

Seeing with what intense anxiety Blanche was gazing at him, Ferrand went on to say, with assumed cheerfulness, " These fellows have made me a sort of judge over them, and as they are willing to carry out almost any orders that I choose to give,—they call me their Commodore. I must go, now, and see what I can do for them."

Accordingly, he went into the other room, and the clamor of the wreckers subsided into something as much like quietness as could be expected from a party of such rude and uncultivated men. Among the articles which they had secured was a trunk belonging to Mrs. Ferrand, and marked with

16

her name, and this was given to her husband
as a part of his share. As usual, there were
articles among the plunder that caused, between certain of the wreckers, disputes which
it taxed all their Commodore's ingenuity
and his patience also to settle. At length,
the division was made, and the wreckers,
some with satisfaction, and some with sulki-
ness,—each carried off his share. Ferrand
and Giles then took hold of Blanche's trunk,
and brought it into the room where she was.

"Well, dear, you and Bessie will have some
clothes now," said the Lieutenant, smiling.

Blanche tried to smile in return, but her
heart was too anxious in regard to a far more
important subject. As soon as Giles had left
the room, she said to her husband, inquir-
ingly,—"And these men are wreckers?"

"Yes;" replied he, "but, Blanche, you
must not suppose,—as many people do, —that

a man cannot be a wrecker without being a robber!"

"Oh," said Blanche, with an accent of distress, "the very conversation of those men shows that they are wicked, lawless, and hardened;—and it bewilders me to try to think how you, Frank, can be willing to live among such people."

Ferrand had expected some such remonstrance as this, and yet, when it came, it cut none the less deeply. Throwing himself into a chair, with that affected carelessness of manner with which people sometimes try to hide real despair, he said, "I cannot help it. I would rather get my living and yours from wreckers, than from certain kind relations of ours. I have failed in everything, and now, we cannot be so fastidious."

"Dear Frank, don't say so! I care nothing for a large house, fine furniture, or costly

dresses;—for as long as we have free con-
sciences, unspotted names, and the right to
claim God as our friend, I feel that we are
rich, and I am happy. But to lose our
peace within,—our self-respect,—to lose the
privilege of asking God to help us, even in
our extremest need,—Oh, that is poverty!"

As Blanche spoke thus earnestly, she held
her husband's hand clasped in both of hers,
and large bright drops, from the heart's inmost fountains flowed rapidly down her
cheeks. Ferrand was deeply moved, and
yet he thought it would heighten his wife's
distress if he owned that he was really engaged in a pursuit which went against his
conscience. Neither would he let her know
under what circumstances he had become the
leader of the wreckers. He knew that it
would only increase her horror of them to
be told that when he was first thrown

among them, they had plundered him of
everything, and threatened to hang him.
While he was casting about in his mind for
something to say, there was a rap at the room
door. Mrs. Ferrand wiped away her tears,
and the Lieutenant went to the door, and
opened it.

Mrs. Giles was there, and she informed
the Lieutenant that a lady, who had escaped
from the wreck, wished to see Mrs. Ferrand.
The lady was immediately invited to come
in, and proved to be a Mrs. Stillingwell,
whom Blanche had found, during the voyage, a very pleasant and intelligent acquaintance. They met now, as old and intimate
friends meet, after being long parted,—so
gladdening was it to see any survivor from
last night's scene of death. Yet Mrs. Stillingwell had a sorrowful story to tell. Her
eldest son, a lad of seventeen, had been with

her on board the steamer, and had perished.
But he was a Christian youth, one of that
noble " Sabbath-school army," who in life,
are Christ's soldiers,—in death, His witness-
es.   His mother knew that, from the dark
waves of a stormy ocean, he had risen to be
with those of whom it has truly been sung,

" Their sorrows now are o'er;
The sea is calm, the tempost past.
On that oternal shore."

Yet, there was one seemingly trifling incident, which that morning had sent a pang
through the freshly wounded and still
bleeding heart of the bereaved mother. Her
son, when he was drowned, had on a beautiful watch chain, which he greatly prized, and
which he had received from his mother as a
birth-day gift, two years before. While on
her way to see Mrs. Ferrand, Mrs. Stillingwell noticed this chain, which her dead boy

had so dearly valued, worn as a necklace by a sun-burned, rough-haired, bare-footed girl of fourteen, who said that her mother got it for her, after the wreck. Mrs. Stillingwell told the girl that this chain had belonged to her son, and begged that it might be restored to her, but "Spunky Poll," as she was generally called, answered by a rude and saucy refusal. Mrs. Stillingwell sobbed bitterly as she related this affair to Mrs. Ferrand, and Blanche felt for her the sincerest sympathy.

"Perhaps you can do something in this case, Frank," said Blanche to her husband.

"I shall be very willing to try," answered Lieutenant Ferrand, and he immediately sent "Spunky Poll," and her mother, a request that they would come for a few minutes, to Giles's cottage. In a short time they came, and after nodding to Lieutenant Ferrand, stared at his wife with intense curiosity. Little Bessie, having taken one look at these strangers, ran and hid her face in her mother's lap, alarmed by their wild and rough appearance. Polly's mother was bare-footed also, and never at any season of the year wore any covering upon her head except her coarse hair, which hung down her back in a sort of loosely twisted rope. Her face was roughened by exposure to all kinds of weather, but this was a mere trifle compared with the unpleasantness of her expression, which was harsh, and forbidding in the extreme.

Lieutenant Ferrand had always been considered as having more than common powers of persuasion; and he now represented to Polly and her mother, in the most moving manner, the anxiety which Mrs. Stillingwell felt to take home with her the keepsake belonging to that son whom she had just lost.

Polly, however, clutched the chain with a greedy look which showed that nothing could weigh with her against the possession of so fine an ornament ; and her mother said, " Pshaw, Lieutenant, don't try to get around us with all this palaver! I waded out into the breakers at day-light this morning, and got that chain off the dead body, that didn't care no more about chains nor nothing;—and so it was mine, 'cordin' to all the wrecker's rules, and now I've give it to Poll, it's *hern*."

"Well, Polly," said the Lieutenant, "I will buy this chain, if you will sell it to me. You know the yacht is going to start off this morning, and when it comes back I shall have some money. A string of red beads would be much more becoming to you than that chain is, and by selling it to me, you can get enough money to buy beads, ear-rings, and a couple of gay dresses."

Polly was silent for a moment, and then, in the tone of one who felt herself to be much persecuted, she whimpered out, " But I'd rather have this."

"So you *shall* have it," said her mother with a fiercer look and tone ; " I didn't get it for you to sell, and, if you let anybody coax you out of it, I'll give you the awfullest pounding that you ever had !"

Mrs. Stillingwell, during this conversation, had been sitting in the farthest corner of the room, with her face turned to the wall, and she now said faintly, without looking round, " Lieutenant, it is useless for you to take any more trouble about the matter. Let these people go away."

At that moment, a new idea struck Mrs. Ferrand. Forgetting her weak and wearied state, she rose hastily from her chair, went to the trunk which had been returned to her that morning, and kneeling down before it, opened the lock by pressing a skillfully contrived spring. She then brought out a long and very elegant gold chain, and, holding it up, said to Ferrand, " Frank, this was one of your gifts to me, and I cannot part with it except by your consent, but I know you will consent for me to ransom with it that chain of Mrs. Stillingwell."

" Certainly, dear, and I shall think all the more of you for being willing to give it up, for such a purpose as that," answered the Lieutenant.

Polly and her mother both saw at once, that Mrs. Ferrand's chain was a greater prize than that which belonged to young Stillingwell, but they were perfectly astonished at what they considered the lady's folly and simplicity, in making such a sacrifice. Polly strutted triumphantly away, with Blanche's chain around her neck, and Mrs. Stillingwell held in her hands, and pressed against her heart, the loved memento of her dead son. She felt so much gratitude and attachment to Blanche that it seemed almost impossible to part from her, and yet she was obliged very soon to tear herself away. She and the other survivors of the wreck, were to go, that morning, on board of Ferrand's yacht, and be conveyed to the nearest town upon the coast

After Mrs. Stillingwell had gone, Blanche reflected, in silence, for a little while, upon the incident which we have just related, and then she exclaimed, in a tone of sorrowful significance, " Oh, Frank, if even the women and children among these wreckers are so hardened, what must the men be ?"

But Ferrand now brought up the excuse which Giles had suggested to him when he first came to Florida, and assured his wife that he wished to stay among the wreckers, for a while, with the hope of making them better. Now, Blanche knew that nothing could effect this except the power of gospel faith, and that as her husband himself was not under its influence, he could not be expected to lead others to Jesus. But she only said, "Well, dear, if you set about that good work in Christ's name, and in God's own way,—it may prove successful."

At the same time, however, she could not repress a sigh, which betrayed her fear that he was building upon a false foundation. Ferrand himself, as we have seen, had begun to doubt very strongly that he could do much towards reforming the wreckers, and he evasively replied, "My promise only binds me

17

to stay here for one year.—But, what will you and Bessie do, during that time? There is no suitable home for you in this wild place, and among these rough people."

"I am resolved to stay here as long as you do," answered Mrs. Ferrand; "and it was with that intention that I came to Florida, to seek you."

Finding that this was Blanche's determination, Lieutenant Ferrand immediately set about providing her with a more pleasant, and more retired dwelling-place than Giles's cottage.

They were talking over the subject that afternoon, when Marianna came again, with a large bouquet of flowers for Mrs. Ferrand, and a smaller one for Bessie. When Blanche informed her of what she and the Lieutenant had been talking, Marianna exclaimed, "How delightful it would be, if you would

come and live in our house, on the island."
Mrs. Ferrand could see the island from her
room windows, and she thought that it would
indeed be a charming dwelling-place. The
Lieutenant remarked to Marianna, with a
smile, "I know that your grandfather could
not find any accommodations in his house for
me; but I wish that you could take Blanche
and Bessie as boarders."

"Ah, yes!" said Marianna, "And who
knows but that such a thing may be?—
I shall try what can be done, anyhow. I
am going to persuade grandfather with all
my might, and I will do more than that;—I
will pray that we, who suit each other so
well, may have a home together."

Lieutenant Ferrand smiled at this, but
Blanche, with a look of earnest approval,
murmured, "Yes, dear Marianna."

After tea, that evening, Marianna sat

down beside her grandfather, and told him all about the rescue of Mrs. Ferrand and her child from the ocean, on the preceding night. The old man said nothing, but seemed to be absorbed in smoking his large pipe, with its porcelain bowl and ebony stem;— yet Marianna knew that he listened to her, for anything like news was welcome when it came to one who led such a tedious life as did Von Ulden.

"The little girl" continued Marianna, "is nearly the age that I was, when we were shipwrecked on this coast. It would have put you in mind of that time grandfather, if you had seen the little child when she was brought into Giles's cottage, in her night dress, all drenched with salt water."

"I can remember 'that time,' well enough," drily, yet not harshly, answered the old man.

"And Mrs. Ferrand," said Marianna, "seems to me to be very much like what I can remember of my mother. Didn't mother have soft brown hair, a pale complexion, and a sweet heavenly look?"

"Yes," answered Von Ulden, in his mildest tone, — for never had any creature been more dear to him than his amiable and affectionate daughter-in-law, Marianna's mother.

After a short pause, Marianna went on to say, "Grandfather, since I've seen Mrs. Ferrand, I've been thinking how nice it would be if I could have her company every day. You know I have never had any companions, because you didn't wish me to associate with the girls about here,—but she is so different from all these people. And the little child is so pretty, and cunning, and playful, that it is a perfect treat just to watch her, and listen

17*

to her! Now, grandfather, there is no suitable place about here for Mrs. Ferrand and Bessie to live, unless they come to board with us, and Mrs. Ferrand says that she would be delighted if they could do so."

Up to this point, Von Ulden had listened to his granddaughter with a great deal of patience, but now, taking the pipe out of his mouth, and staring at her with angry astonishment, he exclaimed, "What,—have the wife and child of that jackanapes Ferrand here, so that he may be coming, every day to my house, and putting on airs, in his character of "the new Commodore?"—If I do anything of the kind, I wish I—"

"But listen to me one moment, please, grandfather," said Marianna. "Lieutenant Ferrand doesn't feel proud at all, of being called "Commodore," by the wreckers, and he told his wife, this afternoon, that he really

envied you, for being able to live here, so
quiet and independent."

Von Ulden was somewhat mollified by
this, but answered in a dogged tone, "I don't
care what he says.   I hate the fellow, and I
don't want to see him,   It's just like his im-
pudence, to think of quartering his family in
my house!"

"But grandfather," pleaded Marianna, "it
is for my sake that I want you to let Mrs.
Ferrand come here.   I know that she is just
what you wish me to be, when I grow up,
and, if she was here, I could learn from her
a thousand things that I ought to know, if I
am to be a lady, as she is.   Mrs. Ferrand
would be like a mother, or rather, like an
elder sister, to me, and Bessie would be such
an amusing playmate."

As Marianna finished speaking, she twined

her arms about the old man's neck, and looked up entreatingly into his face.

Von Ulden was perplexed, for he could not help feeling the force of what Marianna had said, in regard to the advantages which she would derive from Mrs. Ferrand's society.

But then came up his dislike to the Lieutenant, and the author of evil suggested that he would be acting weakly if he consented to anything which would please "the new Commodore." So he said to his granddaughter, in the tone of one who wishes to cut short a puzzling argument, "I know what's best for you, and for myself, too. Go to bed, now, and don't plague me any more about these Ferrands."

Marianna with a sigh, bade her grandfather good-night and retired. She felt utterly disappointed, until she remembered

that there was still one resource left,—that
of praying for what she desired.

Next morning, Von Ulden was surprised
to receive a visit from old Giles, who began
a conversation by complimenting him upon
the pleasant appearance of his dwelling. He
then introduced the subject of taking Mrs.
Ferrand and little Bessie to board, and told
Von Ulden that if he would consent to do
this, the wreckers would compensate him by
furnishing enough provisions, of first class
quality, to support his whole family. It was
true, that at present there was not room
enough in the house for any extra occupants,
but Lieutenant Ferrand would pay the expenses of having two additional rooms put
up.

We have shown, in the first part of this
history, that Von Ulden's ruling passion was
avarice,—or the greed of gain;—and the

meanness of this vice is proved by the fact that, for the sake of having all the provisions furnished for his family without any charge, Von Ulden consented to that which he had denied to the entreaties of his granddaughter, the only living being for whom he had any affection! Yet, unexpected as was this turn of affairs, Marianna did not fail to recognize, with joy and gratitude, the ruling hand of that Providence which causes all things to "work together for good to them that love God."

The two additional rooms were quickly put up, and this improvement to his house was another gain on the side of Von Ulden. Nor was there any lack of furniture for the whole house, as Von Ulden had stored up a quantity of articles of that kind, taken from the cabins of wrecked vessels.

In a few days, Mrs. Ferrand and her little

girl came to take up their abode on the island, and their presence in the house formed
a novel and most pleasing change in the life
of Marianna.

CHAPTER X.

IF we were to say that Marianna exerted herself to render Mrs. Ferrand and her child comfortable and happy, we should not be speaking correctly, for it was no exertion to Von Ulden's granddaughter to show every possible kindness and attention to those whose unexpected presence in her house she regarded as such a blessing. It was not Mrs. Ferrand's disposition to give others any trouble, if she could possibly help it, and she sought for ways of making some return for those services which she was

18 (205)

obliged to receive. In former days, Von Ulden had, at different times, secured from the wrecks of vessels, whole bales of dry goods, which furnished an ample wardrobe for Marianna; and there were still stored away in a trunk, three or four pieces of goods which had never been touched by scissors or needle. Marianna, though a very good seamstress in other respects, was no great adept at dress-making, and the woman who did the housework rarely had time to assist her in such matters. But Mrs. Ferrand had plenty of leisure, and she commenced making clothing for Marianna, from the long neglected goods, with a taste and skill which struck the island girl with wonder and admiration.

Whenever Von Ulden met Mrs. Ferrand, he gave a nod of his head, without saying anything, and when she spoke to him, he made a brief though civil reply. Lieutenant Ferrand had given Blanche warning that the old man was surly and eccentric, but she was not aware that Von Ulden had any especial ill-will towards her husband.

About sunset, every day, the Lieutenant came to see his wife and child, and, at that time, Von Ulden took care to be out of the way, so as not to meet with the object of his unreasonable dislike. If they met, by accident, the old man would immediately turn away, without taking the slightest notice of Ferrand, who, in return, pretended to be just as unconscious of his presence,

The Lieutenant had told the wreckers that Mrs. Ferrand was very delicate, and must be kept as quiet as possible, and, accordingly, none of them must ever come to the island to speak with him. If they wished to see him, they should wait until he returned to the main-land.

Ferrand, however, had more than one object in giving this order. He was ashamed of the wreckers, and of his transactions with them, and he wished therefore, to keep them out of Blanche's sight and hearing.

Mrs. Ferrand and Marianna talked a great deal together, and never lost their interest and pleasure in each other's company. It would be hard to tell upon which side the most wonder and admiration were felt, for Mrs. Ferrand was greatly surprised by the language and sentiments of Marianna, when she considered that this girl had been brought up in solitude,—far from schools, from cities, and from all refined and intelligent society.

But Marianna's ignorance was not so great as to benumb the powers of a mind which was at once thoughtful and active. In the

first place, aunt Naomi had made her a constant and zealous student of the Bible. She
had studied out the beauties of its inspired
poetry and its Divine philosophy, and there
was not a scene or a circumstance of her
daily life for which she could not find some
suitable text, expressive of a great and en-
nobling truth.

The only work in verse which Marianna
possessed, was aunt Naomi's hymn-book, and
she had learned by heart every stanza which
struck her as being either beautiful in language or devotional in spirit. Those songs of
Zion which she warbled so untiringly, seemed
like companions to her as she went about her
household tasks, or mused in the orange-tree
bower, or took her lonely walks along the
shore. We have spoken of those works
of modern history which Marianna found
and read so eagerly.

18*

Again and again she wept over the fate of
Lady Jane Grey, and admired the lofty
Christian firmness of Lady Russell. She
read of those Scottish martyrs, "of whom
the world was not worthy," and who, for the
Truth's sake," wandered in deserts, and in
mountains, and in dens and caves of the
earth. Opening the history of her own
country, she missed not a word which told
her how the Huguenot exiles of France, and
the Puritan pilgrims of England, crossed the
ocean to seek upon the shores of America
" Freedom to worship God." Then, Marianna made the acquaintance of all the noble
men and women of our Revolutionary days,
and thought over their words of eloquence
and patriotism, and their heroic and self-
sacrificing acts, until she was so rapt into the
spirit of them that it seemed as though she
herself, had striven, endured, and conquered,

with them. Marianna had found, in an old desk of her grandfather's, a blank book, in which she frequently wrote down remarks upon what she had read, or some of her reflections upon religious subjects, which had proved so pleasant and cheering to her mind that she did not wish to forget them again. Her writing in this book had given Marianna the power of putting her thoughts into words more easily than she could otherwise have done, and words cannot express what a great satisfaction it was to her to have some one to whom she could talk freely and confidentially, as she could to Mrs. Ferrand.

Every day, Blanche was enabled to gratify Marianna's thirst for knowledge by describing to her something of which she had hitherto been ignorant. Nothing interested the young listener more than did Mrs. Ferrand's account of the public worship to which she had been accustomed.—for Marianna had never, within her recollection, been in a church, nor had she ever seen one.

On a certain afternoon, Blanche had been telling her young friend about the different kinds of schools which are provided for children and youth, and which none of us would need to have described for our information. When Mrs. Ferrand paused, Marianna asked, "Are there no other kinds of schools?"

"I cannot think of any others, just now," was the reply, "except the Sunday Schools."

"What are the children taught there!" inquired Marianna.

"The object," replied Mrs. Ferrand, "is to teach them to be Christians. Those who are too young to understand sermons may there learn to know their Saviour, and give their hearts to Him who gave his life for *them.*"

" What books do they use?" was the next question.

" They study the Bible, and, if any other books are used, they are intended only to make the children understand that more clearly."

" And are the naughty children punished there as in other schools that you have been telling me of?"

" Oh, no !—There are no punishments there. Love, and love only, is the ruling power of such a school. The teachers get no pay, except the satisfaction that loving hearts feel in making those around them happier and better ;—and the scholars, even before they learn to love their Saviour, are led to come by a love for their teachers, or their school. Think, Marianna, of hundreds

of children meeting together to learn about
heavenly things, and all joining their voices
in the sweet Sabbath School hymns, making
music that the angels in Heaven might pause
in their songs to listen to!"

Marianna's eyes filled with tears of inex-
pressible delight, as she exclaimed, "Oh,
how happy those children must be!—How
glad they must feel when Sunday comes !—I
wonder if they know that the children here
have no Sabbath School? I do wish that
the time might come when I could be a Sunday School teacher, among these poor children! Yes, I wish that we could try it now;
but I know that neither grandfather nor the
wreckers would listen to such a thing."

Here, the arrival of Lieutenant Ferrand
put a stop, for the present, to this conversation, but the subject of it was to dwell in

Marianna's mind throughout the whole of her succeeding life.

A few weeks after the arrival of Mrs. Ferrand in Florida, little Bessie's birth-day occurred, and it was celebrated by a small select party, consisting of Marianna, Bessie's mother and father, and the little girl herself. They sat down beneath the shade of orange trees, and amidst blooming magnolias, to a really delicious supper of fruit of various kinds, home-made cake, honey in the comb, and rich pure milk. Marianna crowned Bessie with a wreath of white roses, but could not help laughing with Lieutenant and Mrs. Ferrand, to see the change which took place in the little creature's air and demeanor, under the consciousness of "looking pretty." Bessie, however, though the laugh was against herself, joined in it with the most over-flowing good humor, and by hugging and kissing each of the other persons present, proved that she was neither hurt nor offended.

Already, Bessie could talk very distinctly, and every new phrase which she picked up was hailed, both by Marianna and Mrs. Ferrand, with as much delight as though the little one had never said anything "cunning" before. But we have not the time to linger long upon these pleasant subjects, and, in giving a true description of human life, we can never proceed far without being obliged to relate something that has upon it the shade of sadness.

Mrs. Ferrand was naturally of a delicate constitution, and for the last two years, she had gradually been growing more and more fragile. Lieutenant Ferrand expected that, after recovering from that shock which she had endured on the night of the wreck,

Blanche would come back to the same degree of strength and activity which she had, when he last left her, to go upon his West Indian voyage. But, on the contrary, she continually grew weaker and thinner, though she never uttered any complaint, and always returned soothing answers to his anxious questionings as to how she felt.

For some time, Ferrand clung to the hope that the mild and agreeable climate in which she now was living would produce an improvement in Blanche's health, but, gradually the cold chill of disappointment settled over this expectation too. He told his wife that he would go to the nearest city, and get some reliable doctor to come and give an opinion as to her case;—and Blanche calmly replied, that if it was his wish to do so, she gave her full consent.

Ferrand took the proposed journey, and
19

brought back with him the best physician whose services he could procure. After the doctor had held a short conversation with Mrs. Ferrand, the Lieutenant walked with him down to the island shore, and they talked together for some time. At length, Ferrand returned to the apartment where Blanche was sitting alone, while Marianna and Bessie were chasing each other about the garden. His face was pale as marble, and the pupils of his eyes were dilated like those of one who suffers intense pain, yet a cheerful smile was upon his lips, and, in a steady yet gentle tone, he remarked, " The Doctor says you must be very careful of yourself, Blanche."

What a sweetness of expression, what tenderness and sympathy, were in Blanche's looks!

" Come and sit here, Frank," said she.

Ferrand took the chair to which she pointed. "Now, dear," she continued, "why should you put such a constraint upon yourself, and force that smile, when the heart is so full? I cannot but expect that you should be sorry to part with me, after we have been so happy together!"

At these words, Ferrand's false strength suddenly gave way. His head dropped forward, his hands were pressed over his face, and he wept as he had never done since, when a boy, he stood beside his mother's coffin. Those convulsive sobs, which shook his whole frame, seemed like the throes of death, and as they grew fewer and fainter, he uttered words which touched Blanche's heart more deeply than did even his tears.

"I could have borne anything else," he ejaculated. "I have borne humiliations and losses that would have crushed other men ;—

and I have not shed a tear, nor uttered a complaint. But I am conquered now;—I cannot endure this!"

"Yes, dear Frank, God will give you strength to endure it. Oh, it is amazing what we can bear, with His help! I have often felt afraid that I could not be resigned to leaving you and Bessie; but, now that the trial has come, I seem to be braced up by a courage that is not my own, and my heart feels wonderfully calm and cheerful. How true are those two precious texts of Scripture, "My grace is sufficient for thee," and " As thy day, so shall thy strength be!"—Only trust the Lord, dear, and you will find that He can support you in any trial."

Ferrand made no reply, but his heart was not in a state either to receive comfort or to feel resigned. He saw, however, that his grief had drawn from Blanche's eyes tears

which her own situation could not cause to
flow, and he resolved that she should not
again be thus troubled upon his account.
With a struggle, he mastered all outward
signs of emotion; and no mortal eye again
beheld him weep,—no mortal ear heard his
heart's bitter complainings.

As a last resource, Ferrand now betook
himself to prayer, and, for months after this,
he prayed, not only every day, but every
hour of his waking existence. His prayer
was always the same,—" Lord, spare her life!
Restore her to health again!"

He never asked for submission to the will
of God,—whatever that will might be;—and
he did not ask for sustaining grace to support him, in case of Blanche's death. Though
he never put the thought into words, the
spirit of his prayer was this,—"Give me
just what I ask for, or give me nothing!"

When Blanche informed Marianna that the doctor had pronounced her to be in a rapid consumption, the shock to Von Ulden's granddaughter was extremely great. At first, in her despondency, she felt tempted to believe, as Lieutenant Ferrand did himself, that Providence had singled her out to be the victim of special misfortunes. Her mother had early been taken from her,—then her father,—then aunt Naomi,—and now, Mrs. Ferrand was going; and her grandfather was so aged and infirm that his death could not, certainly, be far distant. But unlike the Lieutenant, Marianna steadily resisted, and soon drove from her the thought that God's purposes,—however mysterious they might now appear,—could be any other than those of love and mercy. Yet fain, indeed, would Marianna keep with her that dear friend over whom she had so lately rejoiced as over a new

found treasure, and who was the only
being upon earth into whose sympathizing
ear she could ever pour the full confidence
of her heart. She, too, betook herself to
daily and hourly prayer for Blanche's re-
covery; but her petition breathed the sub-
missive spirit of the Saviour in Gethsem-
ane;—"Father, if it be possible, let this
cup pass from me;—nevertheless, not as I
will, but as thou wilt!"

It was now the chief study, both of Marianna and Lieutenant Ferrand, to do everything possible to render Blanche's life cheerful and pleasant, while she yet remained
with them, and these loving attentions were
well appreciated by the invalid. As she
received the thousand little services of true
affection, a smile of tenderness and pleasure
would beam upon her face, and, at all times
her manner displayed a serene tranquility

which bespoke the soul quiet that reigned within. Her favorite occupations were reading her Bible, doing some useful piece of sewing, or listening to Marianna singing hymns. This last was a source of great pleasure to Bessie also, and the little child would often herself try to sing some of those sweet words to which she listened so attentively.

Grieved as she was at the prospect of losing her friend, Marianna could see that it was not Blanche, but her husband, who was a fit object for pity, and she hoped at first, that Lieutenant Ferrand might find some consolation in watching the blooming health, and innocent playfulness of his little daughter. But in this she was disappointed, for Ferrand was so much absorbed in anxiety for his wife that he now scarcely took any notice of his child. Indeed, it was painful to him to see her thoughtlessly laughing and playing beside her sick mother.

As Blanche's strength began to fail rapidly, the idea struck Marianna, that it might be well to endeavor to prepare Bessie somewhat for an approaching separation from that mother to whose constant presence she had hitherto been accustomed. One day she tried to introduce the subject in talking to that happy and unsuspecting little one, but Marianna's heart failed her, and she burst into tears. At this moment, Mrs. Ferrand, assisted by her husband, came and took her seat beside an open window of her room, which looked into the garden, where the two girls then were. Bessie, with an expression half indignant and half distressed, pointed to the weeping Marianna, and exclaimed, " Look, Mamma,—naughty Minna crying for nothing!"

Blanche, though now unable to leave **her** room, was not confined to her bed, but spent most of the day in a large cushioned easy chair. Three months had now elapsed since her first coming to Florida, when, one morning, Mrs. Ferrand found herself so weak that, after taking a slight breakfast, she was obliged to lie down again upon her bed. Mrs. Giles had, of late, been in the habit of frequently coming over to the island, to assist in attending upon Blanche, and on this occasion she remained with her all day. Lieutenant Ferrand, also, spent the entire day upon the island, and passed the night on a lounge in Von Ulden's sitting-room. The next morning, as her husband was sitting beside her, Blanche drew from beneath her pillow a pocket Bible, bound in faded red and gold, and said, " Frank, I have been wishing to give you some keepsake, and I have chosen this, because it is the most precious thing that I possess. I know that you will love it because it has been so dear to me. When you were away from home, and all our prospects looked dark and clouded, this was my comforter;—and, on that night of the wreck, when I was swept along by the waves, with Bessie in my arms, this book was placed safely next to my heart."

"And, while I live, it shall be kept next to mine," answered Ferrand, with deep emotion, as he received the book, kissed it, and placed it in his bosom.

" I believe it, dear ;" said Blanche, " and I hope that you will sometimes read those pages that I have read so often. Oh, Frank, if, in the darkest hour of your life, you search that book, you will find there the light that you want! If you do not find it at first, look again, and again, for " there is balm in

Gilead, and there is a Physician there." I
know that you will yet come to love the
Bible and the Saviour;—I have prayed for
it so often!"

"You have been my guardian angel, ever
since we first met," replied her husband, fervently. "But don't try to talk any more
just now, dear Blanche. You are weak, and
so much speaking exhausts you."

"Yes, I do feel tired," answered Blanche.
"I will sleep a little now, and, while I am
sleeping, I would like you, Frank, to take a
short walk. You did not stir out of the
house all day yesterday, and you are not
used to such close confinement. Marianna
will sit by me," she added, as Von Ulden's
granddaughter entered the room, with
Bessie.

Lieutenant Ferrand accordingly, bade his
wife an affectionate good-bye, took his hat,

and went out for a little walk, about the island. Bessie now demanded to get up on her mamma's bed, and at Mrs. Ferrand's request, Marianna placed the child beside her mother. Mrs. Ferrand put her arms around her little girl, and in a few minutes, the rosy dimpled child, and the pale, fragile mother, lay sleeping with equal tranquillity. Marianna sat by the bed-side, engaged with some needlework, frequently glancing at the slumbering invalid. Presently Mrs. Ferrand opened her eyes, and fixing them earnestly upon Marianna, said, "That was not a dream!"

"What was it like?" asked Marianna, rising and leaning over the bed.

"Oh, I cannot describe it; such a beautiful scene, and such brightness! I know that it was real, for Jesus has said, "I go to prepare a place for you ;"—and now I have seen that place !"

Her voice sank into a whisper, and she closed her eyes again. Marianna bent over her more closely, gazed at her intently, and then called, "Mrs. Ferrand !"—at first quite softly, and then in a louder, yet more tremulous tone. Finding that she could get no response, Marianna ran to where Mrs. Giles was sitting, in conversation with the hired woman, and begged her to come to Mrs. Ferrand's room. Both of the women came immediately, and after looking closely at Blanche, exclaimed, "Ah, it is all over! She is gone !"

Mrs. Giles gently lifted the sleeping child from the arms of its lifeless mother, and laid it upon a bed in the other room.

Marianna went into the sitting room, and, throwing herself into a chair, wept like a little child. Mrs. Giles followed her, and with well meaning, yet mistaken solicitude, represented to her that " fretting could not do any good," and that she would only make herself sick.

In a few minutes, Lieutenant Ferrand's step was heard in the hall, and Mrs. Giles went to meet him, with a look full of sad significance.

" Don't go up stairs, Lieutenant," said she in a subdued voice, "come in here."

Ferrand followed her into the sitting-room, looked at the weeping Marianna, and sat down in silence.

"I have been telling Miss Marianna," observed Mrs. Giles, " that grieving is all of no use ;—and we all have got to go, sooner or later. I'm sure, them that are gone are better off, for there's nothing but trouble in this world."

After uttering a few more sentences of common place consolation, Mrs. Giles grew silent, for she was getting uneasy and disconcerted under the strangely steady gaze which, all the while, Ferrand kept fixed upon her. It did not seem that he moved an eye-lash, and he appeared to listen to Mrs. Giles as though upon every word she uttered hung an issue more tremendous than that of life or death,—yet, in fact, he did not know what she was saying. Mrs. Giles herself began to suspect this, and after a pause, she asked, "Lieutenant, wouldn't you like to see little Bessie?"

There was no answer, and no change of expression in his countenance. Mrs. Giles came nearer to him and repeated her question. Without a word, Ferrand arose, walked out of the room and immediately left the house.

"Why," said Mrs. Giles, "how strange that man acts!"

She went to the house door, and looked after the Lieutenant until she had seen him go down to the shore, get into a little boat, and row himself across to the mainland. When she returned home, that evening, she was told by her husband that Lieutenant Ferrand had remained locked up in his own room, in their cottage, ever since he returned from the island.

Von Ulden's behaviour, upon the occasion of Mrs. Ferrand's death, was not exactly that which his granddaughter had prepared herself to expect. Though very few words had ever been exchanged between them, the old man had regarded Blanche's presence on the island as a pleasant circumstance; and, on account of her resemblance to Marianna's mother, he would often gaze at her

20*

for a long time, with interest, if he could do
so unobserved. In his mildest tone, he now
remarked to Marianna,—"Well, I am sorry
for this. I was in hopes that Mrs. Ferrand
would be like a mother, and a sister, too, to
you, Marianna,—but I see that you're fated
not to have any suitable friend or companion. You come of an unlucky stock;—
that's certain. She was too good to be the
wife of such a puppy as Ferrand, and if it
had only been him that died, instead of her,
it would have been a great deal more satis-
factory."

After a moment's reflection, Marianna answered, "Oh no, grandfather,—for we are
sure that she has gone to Heaven."

"And Ferrand himself," said Von Ulden,
"is bound to go." With one gesture of distressed entreaty Marianna sprang up and
left the room. It was too shocking and pain-

ful to hear such a judgment pronounced upon another by that hardened and godless
old man, who was himself, every hour, trembling upon the brink of everlasting misery!

CHAPTER XI.

N the morning of the next day after Blanche's departure, Lieutenant Ferrand requested Giles to proceed to the nearest town, and send a telegraphic despatch to Mrs. Ferrand's relatives, so that any of them who desired to do so might be present at her funeral. At the same time, Giles was directed to make arrangements for the burial, which was to take place at a cemetery near the town just mentioned. In order to meet expenses, Lieutenant Ferrand placed in Giles's hands all the money which he then had, and which consisted of his share of the profits from two or three wrecks that had recently taken place.

The next day Ferrand walked out, and directed his steps to the most lonely and secluded spot that he could find. It was about a mile from the wreckers' settlement, and was frequented just enough to keep a narrow path worn through the tall thick grass, and amidst trees and bushes growing in wild luxuriance. No sound was now heard there but the chirping of insects, and the occasional twitter of a bird, as it flew to or from its nest.

"Only a few months ago," thought Ferrand, "how I could have enjoyed such a walk as this! It never required a great deal to make me happy; and, if Fate had only spared her,"—he struck his hand against his breast, and, in doing so, felt the little Bible that Blanche had given him.

"Ah,—she said, that in that book there was comfort for the darkest hour," murmured he. "Surely, my life cannot have a darker hour than this!"

He sat down upon a fallen tree, drew forth the Bible, and opened it, but without any definite object except that of honoring Blanche's last advice. Even from this object his attention was immediately drawn off, by seeing a folded letter placed between the back and blank leaves of the book. It had been written by Blanche in her last illness, and was addressed to himself. She alluded to her approaching departure with tranquillity, and even with cheerfulness, and said everything that piety and love could suggest to render the parting less painful to her husband. She conjured him not to remain among the wreckers longer than the one year for which he was bound by his promise, and begged that, while he was among them, he would exert all the strength of his soul to resist the temptations of such a trying and dangerous position. Indeed, she expressed her opinion, if he found that his present position obliged him to join in, or connive at, what was wrong, he ought to leave the wreckers at once,—since to keep his promise would dishonor him in the sight of God, while to break it, would dishonor him only in the eyes of wicked and lawless men. Finally, Blanche desired that Bessie should remain in Florida as long as her father did, and that, during that time, she should share the home, and be under the care of that dear Christian girl, Marianna Von Ulden.

Ferrand read this letter with all the awe and reverence, the tenderness and emotion, of a person listening to a voice from the beloved dead,—a message from one of the glori-

fied inhabitants of Heaven. About an hour
afterwards, he went to the island, and com-
municated to Marianna Mrs. Ferrand's wish
concerning Bessie. Marianna had feared
that Bessie would speedily be removed from
Florida, and sent to live with some relative
in a distant state, but now, clasping the little
treasure in her arms, she fervently vowed
that, while they remained together, this
child should be the object of her dearest care.

When Mrs. Ferrand's two elder sisters,
with their husbands, came to attend her funeral, they seemed disposed, at first, to insist
upon taking Bessie away, to live with one of
them ; but the Lieutenant's dejection gave
place, for a few moments, to indignation, as
he sternly assured them that no one should
remove the child from the care of that person to whom she had been consigned by a

dying mother's wish, and a living father's authority.

And now Blanche Ferrand is removed from human sight, never more to be seen as a weak, suffering, mortal being. Those of her earthly friends who are privileged to see her again will see her in the resurrection body, blooming and radiant with immortality.

None of the wreckers perceived anything extraordinary in the demeanor of Lieutenant Ferrand after his wife's death. He was serious, thoughtful, and silent,—but this much they had expected. Among all who surrounded him, only the intelligent and sympathizing eye of Marianna could read anything of what was passing in his heart. His calmness was that of a man who has lost everything, and endured the last and worst stroke of misfortune, and who, therefore, has nothing more either to hope or to fear. As for

the kindness of God's purposes, he could no
more realize it, than a Protestant martyr upon the rack could realize the goodness of
the Popish Inquisition. No;—he had merely
set himself down to bear with patience and
dignity the injuries, (for, strangely as it
sounds, this is the feeling of many people in
similar circumstances,) the injuries which
Providence chose to inflict upon him.

Marianna, trusting in God, did not find
herself left to loneliness and sorrow, for the
care of Bessie occupied her mind, while the
child's company cheered her spirits. She
provided Bessie with the same kind of toys
which had amused her own early childhood,
—shells from the sea-beach and acorns from
the grove. Among the wrecks upon that
coast was a little trading vessel called "The
Cherub," which had for its figure-head a
carved wooden representation of the head of

a child, about the size of that of an infant a
year old;—and this head Lieutenant Ferrand
brought with him one day, when he came to
the island to visit his little girl. The wooden
effigy had very blue eyes, very red cheeks,
and a carved imitation of bright yellow hair,
arranged in curls;—and Bessie's fancy was
taken with it immediately. Marianna fixed
to it a small body, made of muslin stuffed
with dried grass, and then dressed it up in
the oldest of Bessie's clothes, when the little
girl joyfully received it in her arms, and
owned it as " her baby."

Bessie, likewise, enjoyed with Marianna
the pleasant company of pretty, harmless,
living things, that willingly bestowed their
society upon those sweet children, whom
they found to be as harmless as themselves.
Birds of song would perch upon the sills of

the open windows near which they sat, and there warble as freely as in the grove.

There was a family of beautiful doves,—of a species peculiar to Florida,—which were so tame that they not only flew around the two girls, when they walked out,—but often, at meal times, came in and alighted upon the edge of the table, to pick up crumbs, and receive other food from the hands of Marianna and Bessie. There were a couple of squirrels, too, that frequently came in at the windows, played around the sitting-room, allowed themselves to be fed by the two girls, and then bounded off to their wild homes again, soon to return for another visit.

But the most interesting hours of Marianna and Bessie were when, early in the morning or late in the afternoon, they walked out together, hand in hand,—generally directing

21*

their steps towards the island shore. Then, while every object around,—from the majestic ocean to the smallest flower-bud,—furnished her with an illustration, Marianna would talk to her little charge of the power and goodness of the great Creator, until by the simple faith of the astonished and admiring child, God's presence was felt pervading every spot of the surrounding sea, earth, and sky. Bessie loved much to hear Marianna tell about the beautiful home to which her mother had gone, and where, some day, they were going, too. In that home, Marianna pictured everything that is most delightful and attractive,—perpetual sunshine,—never fading flowers of magnificent beauty,—glorious mansions,—hosts of happy souls in robes of glittering white,—countless throngs of little children, sporting in continued joy,—the melody of sweet angelic voices, singing their wondrous hymns,—and to complete the whole,—the presence of Jesus smiling tenderly on those He loves so well.

Sometimes Lieutenant Ferrand would accompany Marianna and Bessie in their walks, for theirs was now the only society, within his reach, that he could well endure. Unlike Von Ulden, he had not become so harsh and peevish by his misfortunes as to make all around him unhappy, and the innocent cheerfulness of Marianna and Bessie did not grate upon his feelings as did the rude and depraved mirth of the wreckers.

He assisted his little girl in gathering shells and flowers, and the amiable simplicity of his character increased Marianna's pity for that silent heart-ache which she knew that he endured. He soon began to seek relief from the burden of melancholy thoughts in talking to Marianna of his departed wife,—

in telling how, as a girl, she had walked, with
the serene and lofty indifference of a great
soul, through the "Vanity Fair" of fashion-
able society,—and how, as a wife, her un-
selfish devotion had been as a star that shone
forth the more brightly when the clouds of
adversity gathered around her husband and
her home.

Marianna, as she listened, shed tears of
admiring sympathy, and often expressed the
hope that, in all respects, Bessie might prove
just such a woman as her mother.

One day, as Lieutenant Ferrand, Marianna, and Bessie, sat by the sea-shore, and
watched the waves rolling up on the sand, and
then receding, Ferrand remarked thoughtfully, "This scene, and my own lonely situation, remind me of some lines that were
written by a man who lived somewhere in
Florida;

" My life is like the print of feet
Left upon Tampa's desert sand ;
Soon as the rising tide shall beat,
Those tracks shall vanish from the land.
Yet, as if grieving to efface
All vestige of the human race,
On that lone shore loud moans the sea,
But none shall e'er lament for me !

My life is like the Autumn leaf
That flutters in the moon's pale ray ;
Its hold is frail, its state is brief,
Restless, and soon to pass away.
Yet, ere that leaf shall fall and fade,
The parent tree shall mourn its shade ;—
The winds bewail the leafless tree,—
But none shall breathe a sigh for me !"

There was silence for a few moments, and
then Bessie spoke up, "Papa, that's pretty
talk; but don't say it any more. It makes
Minna's eyes so weak!"

Marianna now began to speak of her own
peculiar heart-trials, beginning with the early

loss of her mother, of whom her faint, yet almost adoring remembrance, was, as she herself said, "Like a dream of an angel!"

This led Lieutenant Ferrand to talking of his mother, who, like Marianna's and Bessie's, had died a holy and a happy death,—so that, in the minds of all those three,—the Naval officer, the young girl, and the little child,— the names of "mother" and "Heaven" were inseparably connected. In such a conversation it was very easy for Marianna to introduce the subject of a future life. She said that she had always felt the truth of what aunt Naomi had told her,—that, in Heaven we shall meet and know again the blessed ones who have been dear to us upon earth, and who shall then receive us with a love and joy unspeakable.

"Don't you think so, Lieutenant?" added Marianna.

" Yes;—Oh, yes!" he answered, with an
earnest sincerity that could not be mistaken;
and he fixed his eyes upon the clear blue
heavens, as if half expecting to see his mother
and Blanche looking down upon and watching him with a deathless affection.

" But it is strange," continued Marianna,
" that we can believe so much more easily in
the love of our human friends than in the
love of God, who gave those friends to us at
first, and who will give them back to us, if we
will only accept of the Heaven that he offers
us!"

" It is very easy, Marianna, for such a one
as you to be a Christian," said Lieutenant
Ferrand.

" Oh no;"— replied Marianna, "and what
faith I have has been given to me in answer
to many, many prayers."

" Yes, I suppose your prayers may be

heard, but mine have not seemed to be," returned Ferrand.

"Aunt Naomi used to say that we never can tell whether we have faith or not until God declines to grant us something that we particularly want," was Marianna's answer.

"If we can trust him then, it is the kind of trust he requires. If our faith is not strong enough for that, how can we ever expect it to be followed by everlasting happiness in Heaven, by sharing in the glory of Jesus, and by enjoying again the company of such dear friends as your mother, and Bessie's and mine? They, when they were in this world, bore every trial so sweetly and meekly;—and what right would we have to share their bliss, unless we can prove our faith as they did theirs?"

Ferrand was silent, but every expression in his speaking eyes and sensitive mouth

LIEUTENANT FERRAND'S RETURN.—Page 252

showed that his feelings were both touched and soothed by dwelling upon the thoughts that Marianna had suggested. Yet when, in the course of their next conversation, she proceeded with all possible tact and delicacy, to speak of the importance of immediately securing our salvation, by coming out upon Christ's side, Ferrand made no reply, but hastily rose and began to walk about, as if for exercise and recreation, but with unmistakable disturbance of mind. Of late, he had kept nothing of his share of the wrecker's spoil, except what sufficed to pay his board, but he knew that both he and his child owed their support to those who were often guilty of acts of dishonesty and cruel wrong. Having met with nothing but failure in his attempt to reform the wreckers, Lieutenant Ferrand had given up the idea, in despair, and thus he seemed to sanction, or

22

connive at conduct which he detested in his soul. The hallowed teachings of a Christian mother had implanted in his heart enough of religious sensibility to make him feel that he was living contrary to conscience, and that, while he thus lived, it was impossible to make any sincere profession of religion. Why, then, did he not, as Blanche had recommended, leave the wreckers at once? Because he had not the moral courage to break a promise which he now saw it was wrong for him ever to have given.

Four months had now elapsed since Mrs. Ferrand's death, and the Lieutenant said to himself, "In three months more, the year will be up, and then I shall be out of this snare. Then, I will have a chance to become as good as any one!"

But Ferrand's case was to afford a sad warning against too great, though very common dangers. The first of these consists in putting off the performance of good resolutions, and the second in being found in bad company. On a certain occasion, Giles and several others of the wreckers, had taken a voyage, in Lieutenant Ferrand's yacht, to the nearest South American port, in order to dispose of some articles which they knew would there find a ready sale. As they returned, they saw a vessel in distress, and about sinking. She proved to be from Brazil, and had on board quite a large sum of money belonging to the Brazilian government. Though they saved the lives of the men on board, by receiving them into the yacht, the wreckers laid their hands upon the treasure, and, with much exultation, stowed it away for their own use. The officer of the Brazilian government, in whose charge the money was, loudly demanded its return, and Giles strongly ad-

vised the wreckers not to keep it, but neither
threats nor persuasions could induce them
to give up their booty.   On this affair being
reported to the Brazilian government, it was
decided that the crew of the yacht were
pirates, and orders were given to seize them
at the first opportunity.   A few weeks afterwards, the commander of the sunken Brazilian
vessel was cruising about in another ship,
when he again encountered the wrecker's
yacht.   This time, Lieutenant Ferrand was
on board, and in command. He knew nothing of the heavy robbery which his crew had
committed, as they had purposely kept the
affair a secret from him ;—and therefore, he
was quite indignant when the Brazilians
boarded his yacht, and ordered himself and
crew to surrender, as pirates.   The wreckers
made a stout resistance, but the other party
had too great an advantage in numbers.   Fer-

rand beheld his crew falling around him, either dead or severely wounded,—with the exception of two half grown boys, who jumped overboard and swam to a neighboring point of land. The Lieutenant himself was overpowered, dragged on board the Brazilian vessel, and thrown upon the deck so roughly as to stun him for a few moments. He was then subjected to the painful and mortifying process of having his hands and feet tightly tied together with coarse ropes, and was put into the vessel's hold, where, thus cruelly tied, he remained all night, and until a late hour the next morning. So unexpected was this misfortune, that Ferrand was completely astonished and bewildered by it, and his only distinct sensations were those of bodily pain and indignation at the manner in which he was treated. The next morning, they reached Rio Janeiro, and Lieutenant Ferrand was

22*

put upon trial, as a pirate. This charge of course, he denied, but acknowledged that he was the commander of the wrecker's yacht and the leader of its crew. One thing alone saved him from a speedy and ignominious death, and that was the fact that no one could testify to having seen him on board of the yacht on the occasion when the Brazilian government's money was taken. It was rather a perplexing case, but the authorities before whom he was tried had no doubt of Ferrand's being a pirate, and he was sent to prison to await a second trial.

And now, Lieutenant Ferrand found himself a solitary prisoner, in a gloomy chamber, with walls and floor of stone, in one of the highest stories of a grim old castellated fortress. In a few days, his desire for freedom became almost maddening and he longed for his second trial, whatever its result might be.

But, in answer to his repeated questionings, the jailor at length told him that he would, most probably, never be tried again, but would be kept imprisoned for the rest of his life, as a dangerous person, who was unfit to be at liberty.

CHAPTER XII.

THE two lads who, as we have mentioned, contrived to escape from the
captured yacht, made their way back
to Florida, with the sad and tragic story
which they had to relate. There was seen,
among the wives and families of the slain
wreckers, every form of wild and boisterous
grief,—often verging upon frenzy, in its utter
hopelessness and lack of any heavenly consolation. Marianna now bitterly reproached
herself with not having had the courage
plainly and directly to urge Lieutenant Ferrand to seek his soul's salvation, while she

had an opportunity to do so,—an opportunity that now, in all probability was gone forever. For a while, she tried to comfort herself with the idea with which she often soothed Bessie, saying that she "hoped Papa would soon come back again;" but, as time passed on, she became convinced that Lieutenant Ferrand was either dead or doomed to a long imprisonment. Yet, few indeed are those situations in life in which we have not the resource of prayer, and Marianna wrestled in an agony of supplication, for the unhappy, erring, absent one.

"Lord of Mercy," she would ejaculate, "if he still lives on earth, let him not die without tasting Thy salvation! Whatever fate awaits his mortal body, give eternal life unto his soul; and Oh, let not the prayers of his sainted mother and wife, or even these weak, unworthy petitions of mine, be poured out to Thee in vain!"

But, keen and torturing indeed was the remorse that now seized upon Giles. He did not forget,—he could not forget, until the latest moment of his life,—that his persuasions and representations had induced Lieutenant Ferrand to take the leadership of the wreckers, and thus had drawn upon him his present misfortune,—ending, perhaps, in an untimely death.

As might have been expected, Giles had not found his own conscience relieved by inducing another person to take the outward responsibility of commanding the wreckers, and now, all the accumulated transgressions of years seemed at once to press upon him, with a crushing weight.

One morning, when Marianna entered Giles's cottage, she found the old sailor sitting with his elbows supported upon his knees, his head upon his hands, and weeping like a child.

Mrs. Giles was much affected by such an outbreak of emotion as she had never known her husband to give way to before, and she sat near him, endeavoring to dry with her check apron the drops of sympathy which flowed from her own eyes. Marianna dreaded that she was to be told some sad news, and tremblingly inquired, " Have you heard anything of the Lieutenant?"

"No," groaned Giles, " but I expect that he's dead, and I wish I was too;—though I'm a fool to wish that, for, if I was to die, I know that I'd go straight down to everlasting torment!"

Marianna could only answer such words as these by telling him of a Saviour's love and mercy, and urging him to pray that his sins might be washed away by the blood shed on Calvary.

"Ah, I wouldn't know how to go about praying," answered Giles, "but, if I could hear you pray for me,—then I might try."

Marianna had never prayed aloud in the hearing of any person but little Bessie, and she felt a natural shrinking from the idea of attempting it in the presence of Giles and his wife;—but then she thought, "It was this cowardice that kept me from talking to Lieutenant Ferrand as I should have done, and I ought to take warning, now, against committing the same mistake another time."

Accordingly, asking God to give her strength, she knelt down, and prayed that this repentant man, and his wife also, might be enabled to avail themselves of that remedy for sin which Jesus has provided. Marianna's prayer was short, but very much to the

23

point, and such was its effect upon Giles, that as soon as she concluded, he fell upon his knees, bowed his head, and clasping his hands together, exclaimed, " Yes, good Lord, forgive my sins, and help me, after this, to live in such a way as to show that I'm really sorry for them! I don't dare to ask it except for Christ's sake. Amen."

Completely overcome by hearing such words proceed from her husband's lips, Mrs. Giles cried out, "Oh, pray for me too!"— Marianna, rejoiced and encouraged by Giles's prayer, immediately complied with the request.

An old Bible, which had long been hidden away in dust and neglect, was now hunted up, and, assisting them to find some chapters which seemed especially suited to their case, Marianna left Giles and his wife to draw strength and comfort from its pages. The

next day she again went to the old sailor's
cottage, but found only Mrs. Giles at home.
She stated that her husband had gone to see
another wrecker, whose eldest son had been
killed at the time of Lieutenant Ferrand's
capture;—and Giles wished to pour into the
afflicted father's heart that balm of Divine
love and mercy whose healing power he himself had just discovered. Marianna found
Mrs. Giles herself filled with the trembling
joy of one who, in olden days, touched the
hem of the Saviour's garment, and found her
malady healed at once, yet scarcely dared to
believe that the Lord would look on her with
favor.

"This is a solemn time among our people,"
she remarked, "but, if there was only any
sorrow for sin mixed with it, the mourning
of many a one would soon be turned into
gladness!"

"As I lay awake last night," said Marianna, "I kept thinking that this would be the very time to start a Sunday-school here."

It had been so many years since Mrs Giles had even heard the name of a Sunday-school, that scarcely anything could have sounded more novel and startling to her than did this suggestion of Marianna. She owned that "Such a thing would be very nice indeed, if it could be done,"—but it was evident that she thought the scheme rather wild and visionary. Marianna replied that she considered such an object worth trying for, at any rate, and she was willing to take the burden of the first trial upon herself, if Mrs. Giles would only second her efforts. The promise to do this was honestly, yet timidly given, and, as soon as Marianna left the cottage, she commenced a round of visits to the women of the wrecker families.

The first upon whom she called was Mrs. Clarke,—the young woman who, when she brought some fish to the island, had conveyed to Marianna the news of the wreck of Lieutenant Ferrand's yacht, and the death of John Ross. By the recent calamity on board that same vessel, Mrs. Clarke had now lost her husband. Marianna found her sitting with her infant child upon her lap, and another little boy, a few years older, playing about the room. A moody dejection appeared in the widow's looks and attitude, and, immediately after inviting Marianna to take a seat, she began to talk of her recent loss.

"All that I can think of," she exclaimed with dry and burning eyes, "is to have my husband's death revenged, and it shall be revenged, yet!"

"On whom would you revenge it?" asked Marianna, "On the Brazilians?"

23*

"Yes, indeed. The blood-sucking wretches. Oh, I could"—

"Yes, interrupted Marianna, "but the Brazilians are completely out of our reach, for, now, we have no vessel that can venture far from the coast. The best thing that we can do is to be revenged on the cause of this sorrowful misfortune."

"What is that?"

"Why, it is this way that our people have of taking things away from their rightful owners, and sometimes ill-treating the owners, if they want their property back again," answered Marianna.

"Well," returned the widow, moodily, "since this has happened to my husband, I don't care what any one else does, or what becomes of them!"

"Yes,—here are these two dear little boys of yours, that I hope will grow up to be a

joy and comfort to their mother's heart.
Would you not like to see them come to be
honest, respectable men, whom no one could
dare to call "pirates," or "thieves?" Then,
if they should never break the laws, their
country would protect them against the Brazilians, or any body else, and would make that
person pay dearly that should dare to raise
a hand against their lives!"

"Indeed, I wish it could be so;"—answered
the mother, as she looked at her children;
"but I suppose they will grow up to be just
like the other wreckers."

"No," said Marianna, "Mrs. Giles and I
are going to try to do something for the
children of this place, to save them from such
dangers as their fathers have perished by.
Next Sunday, I mean to gather the boys and
girls in Mrs. Giles's house and teach them
good things out of the Bible, that will be

useful to them all their lives. Wont you let your little Johnnie come, Mrs. Clarke?"

Marianna asked this question with undissembled anxiety, and, after a moment's pause, was rejoiced to hear the frank response, "Yes, to-be-sure. It can't hurt him, anyhow!"

Having gained this much, Von Ulden's granddaughter proceeded to visit another woman who had lost near relatives when the yacht was captured, and some of those who had not,—were easily convinced that they ought to accept the late calamity as a warning to train up their children in a better way than that which the elder generation had pursued. Others of a more careless disposition, gave their consent also, partly to oblige Marianna, and partly because, as one of them said, she "s'posed it would be some fun for the young ones."

The fathers, as a general thing, seemed to regard it as a matter of not much consequence one way or the other. So long as they themselves were not required to attend upon any religious service, they were content. But some of the parents, when they accepted Marianna's offer, did so with a hearty satisfaction; for there are few fathers and mothers so ignorant, or so hardened, as not to be capable of forming a wish that their children may be wiser and better than themselves. At some of the wrecker's cottages, however, Marianna had to talk a good deal before she could effect her object, and both her grandfather and Bessie complained so much when she stayed long away from home, that two or three days elapsed before she could get through with all her visits.

Each visit from Marianna was followed up on the succeeding day, by one from Mrs.

Giles, whose conversation was directed to the same object, and whose words, simple and unpolished as they were, had great weight with the neighbors.

The boys and girls, when asked if they wished to go, almost always said " Yes," out of curiosity to see to what a Sunday-school was like.

The first Sabbath, Marianna had quite an encouraging attendance of children,—from four years old to fourteen, in Giles's sitting-room, and Bessie Ferrand occupied a chair by the youthful teacher. Bessie was the only scholar who had on shoes or stockings; and those restless bare feet, which were almost continually kicking and flourishing about, were all unwashed,—for very few of their owners had even clean faces or hands. So far from any of these children ever having attended a Sunday-school before, they had

never heard of such an institution, and it
may be easily imagined that Marianna herself knew very little about the way in which
these schools are managed. The children
spoke aloud to each other, without hesitation,
about whatever came uppermost in their
minds. There was considerable laughing
and playing, and many complaints of pinch-
ings, pushings, and strikings, followed by
threats to pay back these injuries, when the
Sunday-school was over. Marianna, however,
was neither surprised nor discouraged by all
this, but thought herself sufficiently fortunate
in being able to gain the attention of her wild
flock, whenever she spoke to them.

She commenced by singing a hymn, to
which all the children listened with absorbed
and pleased attention; but, when she endeavored to teach them the words, their rustic
bashfulness would not permit them to attempt

to sing. Marianna then read aloud a chapter from the New Testament, giving clear and simple explanations as she went along, and she was gratified to hear some of the children asking questions in regard to what had been read,—though it took a good deal of time to answer those questions fully and plainly enough to make herself understood. But these scholars could not get any lessons, because none of them could read, and very few even knew their letters. Marianna saw that this ignorance was a great obstacle, and, therefore, she spent the most of the first Sunday-school session in giving her scholars instruction in the alphabet, or in easy spelling.

Next Sunday, on hearing little Bessie join Marianna in singing a simple hymn, some of the most ambitious pupils were convinced that they, also, must have the ability to learn to sing it, and they made considerable progress in that one afternoon. The rest of the scholars followed their example, and Marianna then gave them texts of Scripture to commit to memory from her dictation. We can easily believe that it was hard work for this young girl to teach a school in which the scholars had no books, and could not have used them if they had; and where she was obliged to repeat over and over everything which she wished her pupils to learn ;—yet she thought herself fully compensated by the progress which they made.

The wreckers and their wives began to regard their children as prodigies, when they heard them singing hymns, and repeating what they had learned on the Sabbath; and, in order to have the satisfaction of seeing and hearing them in the very act of acquiring this wonderful knowledge, many of the mothers and some of the fathers now came

24

in, and remained as spectators and listeners, during the Sabbath-school exercises.
They were silent and respectful, for they
felt astonished at the energy and tact of Marianna, and were touched by the love and
patience which inspired her in her work.

A young woman,—the daughter of one of
the wreckers,—who had always been remarkable for her seriousness and quiet disposition,
was so charmed with Marianna's work that
she volunteered to assist her in it, and it soon
became evident that she was taught of God
for this purpose. Finding that the whole
settlement was becoming interested in the
Sunday-school, Giles set to work and collected
a Bible-class of men, and Mrs. Giles,—though
with much trembling and self-distrust,—suffered herself to be persuaded to become the
teacher of a little band of women.

The progress of the Sunday-school was attended by a corresponding reform in the grown people of the wrecker community. Samuel Giles was now the man who had most influence and authority among the wreckers, and he was resolved, henceforth, to walk in the fear of God. For awhile, he did not explain to his companions the exact nature of the resolutions which he had taken ; nor did he urge them, in so many words, to pledge themselves to a new course of conduct. He preached to them only by his daily example, by actions of humanity, honesty, and self-sacrifice,—by frequent references to God, as being both the witness and the judge of all things,—and by reading his Bible, and holding domestic worship, with his wife,—regardless of contemptuous or disapproving beholders. When any man seemed serious or impressed, Giles took the opportunity of telling him how, through

the merit of atoning blood, we may become
heirs to the riches of God in Christ Jesus.
Marianna used all her powers of mind to
win the females of the settlement to love the
beauty of holiness; and Mrs. Giles, though
naturally a woman of few words, could always clearly and distinctly bear witness to
the truth, when she felt it her duty to do so.
That divine and mysterious power which
was, at first, a hidden leaven, worked gradually and noiselessly, until, at length, its effects might have been seen by any eye. Some
of the wreckers openly testified their repen-
tance for past wickedness, and embraced
the Saviour's offers of pardon. The Sabbath
was generally observed;—shipwrecked people were treated with kindness and humanity;
and it now came to be considered a disgrace-
ful thing for any wrecker to keep possession

of goods whose lawful owner was present to claim them.

We have related these pleasing changes with some rapidity, but it must not be supposed that they were the growth of a few days. The degree of progress which we have just described, was not reached until nearly two years after the capture of Lieutenant Ferrand. During that time, no tidings of the unfortunate prisoner reached the ears of any one who took an interest in his fate, and the people of the wrecker settlement always spoke of him as one who was numbered with the dead.

Bessie was now a lovely and intelligent child of six years, and, as she grew older, instead of gradually losing the remembrance of her father, she dwelt upon his loss with a deeper regret, and cherished more fondly the dim hope that he might yet be restored to her. Not a night or a morning came, but Bessie, with folded hands and up-lifted gaze, knelt and prayed,—as Marianna had long since taught her,—that God would give her father back to her, even on this earth, or, if this was not the Divine will, that she might meet him, at last, among the glorified in Heaven. Very often did Bessie and Marianna sit beside the island shore, and talk of Lieutenant Ferrand, until both of them, sinking into silence, would remain gazing across the sea, as if in the hope of seeing some vessel appearing on the distant waves, to bring back the absent and lamented one.

It was at the time of which we are now speaking, that a stranger, or a person who, at first appeared to be such, arrived at the wreckers' settlement. He was a tall youth of respectable and prepossessing appearance, who would have been supposed, from the

manliness of his figure and bearing, to
number at least twenty-one years, though
in reality he was but little over eighteen.
The first person he enquired for was Lieutenant Ferrand, and on hearing the little
that was known of his fate, he covered his
face with his hands and wept in an agony of
grief and disappointment. This conduct
caused a number of persons to gather around
and gaze at him, and a new surprise awaited
them when they learned that they were now
looking once more upon the long absent
Hugh Ross!

Giles immediately invited the youth to his
cottage, where Marianna and Bessie happened
to be visiting Mrs. Giles. Marianna cordially greeted Hugh when she learned who
he was,—for she would certainly not have
known him without an introduction.

Hugh recognized her at once,—for with

the exception of having grown to a womanly
height, she had changed but little in appearance since he last saw her.

"I see," said Hugh, "that joy and grief
are mixed in every scene of our lives. The
first person whom I spoke with, on coming
back to this place, told me most sorrowful
and unwelcome news;—but this is a happy
moment, when I have a chance at last, of
thanking you, Miss Marianna, for all that you
have done for me!"

"I never knew," said Marianna, "that I
was privileged to do anything for you."

"Yes," exclaimed Hugh, "it was you who
first told me of a Saviour;—it was you who
gave me this Bible, and bade me look into it
whenever I wished to know that Saviour's
will, so that I might guide my conduct accordingly. This Bible, ever since then, has
been my counsellor, and a " lamp to my feet."

By clinging to its principles, in the midst of every temptation, I have gained the friendship of the good and generous, who contributed of their means to educate me for a minister of the gospel. I have finished my first term at the theological seminary, and I have taken advantage of this vacation to do what I have long intended,—come here, and see if I can accomplish anything for the souls of the wreckers."

"And do these Christian people, who are educating you, pay for your board, clothing and traveling expenses?" asked Giles.

"No," said Hugh, I neither expect nor wish them to do that. During the college terms, I devote my spare hours to copying for lawyers, and in vacation, I act as a colporteur, going about selling religious books, and getting subscribers for religious newspapers. I am very thankful indeed to be able to earn my own living, and pursue my studies, at the same time, and if the Lord will bring me into the gospel ministry, and bless my labors in it, I ask for nothing more!"

Marianna,—as was generally the case, when she went away from home,—had been obliged to promise her grandfather that she would soon return, and, after a little more conversation in regard to Hugh's future work, she rose to depart. Bessie had been out upon the beach, gathering shells and curious pebbles, but, at Marianna's call, she now came bounding into the cottage.

"Why, what sweet little girl is this?" asked Hugh, taking the child's hand.

"Whom does she look like?" said Marianna."

"She has Lieutenant Ferrand's eyes," replied Hugh, turning pale with emotion.

Marianna then told him of the coming of

Lieutenant Ferrand's wife and child to Florida, and of Mrs. Ferrand's death,—circumstances with which Hugh was unacquainted, as they had taken place since his departure from that neighborhood. This story was, to young Ross, a very interesting and affecting one, and, at its conclusion, he clasped Bessie to his bosom with a fervor that startled her.

"My heart will never be at rest," exclaimed Hugh, "until I have found out the fate of this dear child's father, and until I have tried to do something in his behalf, if he is yet alive."

Giles declared that Hugh must be his guest while he remained in Florida, and young Ross slept that night in the room which had formerly been occupied by Lieutenant Ferrand, and where the wrecker's orphan boy had bidden farewell to his earliest friend, before he went forth, alone, into the world.

The next day was Sunday, and Hugh was much surprised, that afternoon, to see all the children, and a majority of the grown people in the settlement, come thronging into Giles's house. Marianna and Bessie were among the earliest arrivals. Marianna greatly enjoyed Hugh's unspeakable astonishment, when he found that here was really a Sunday-school,—and a flourishing one too,—in the wreckers' village. By the time the exercises closed, young Ross had sufficiently recovered from his bewilderment to address those who were there present, and to endeavor to tell them something of the joy which he felt at seeing what God had wrought among them. He told the wreckers' children that he had been one of themselves, and one of the poorest and most neglected boys in the

wrecker settlement; but that while he remained in his native place, no Sunday-school
had ever opened for him those kindly doors
which welcome the humblest and most despised. He was quite a tall boy when he last
left the settlement, and went to Tallahassee,
but he had become one of the scholars of a
Sunday-school in that city, and by the instructions which he there received, had
learned to understand more and more fully
the teachings of that Bible which was his
only guide and counsellor. When he left
Tallahassee, and went to another city, to take
a situation in a store, he immediately joined
another Sunday-school, and it was his teacher
there who had set on foot a movement,
among the wealthy members of the church,
to have him educated for the ministry. Having thus related his story to the listening

25

children, Hugh addressed himself to the grown people present.

"Your Sunday-school," said he, "has got so far that it is time for it to go a good deal farther. Already, this room is so crowded that it is neither pleasant nor convenient, and soon it will be impossible to find room for all who wish to come in. Why not set to work and put up a building that will be worthy of the purpose, and a credit to this place?"

This was one of the thoughts that are destined not to die, and be forgotten,—because God sets the seal of His approval upon them, and in their influence and effects they become immortal.

The people talked over the new suggestion, and Marianna and the Gileses gave it all the weight of their hearty approval. By the advice of Giles, three or four of the wreckers had built for themselves small trading vessels, and a couple of these men started for the nearest town upon the coast, to bring home such building materials as were not to be procured near the settlement. Almost all the wreckers gave more or less assistance in putting up the building, and not many weeks after Hugh had first started the idea, it was ready for use. The edifice was one story high, and contained but one room; but this room was spacious enough to wear, in the eyes of the wrecker community, something of an air of grandeur. It was, in truth, a pleasant and airy apartment, with neatly plastered and white-washed walls. Under Hugh's directions, a number of benches, and a reading desk, were made, and arranged in proper order.

On the morning of the next Sabbath, after the completion of the building, Hugh preached in it, the first religious discourse ever publicly delivered upon this portion of the coast of Florida. Curiosity induced a good attendance, and the young theological student adapted the style of his discourse to his auditors, making it plain, clear, pointed, and energetic.

Hugh saw that some of his hearers were seriously impressed, and he felt that there was more hope of these people than of those who, hearing the gospel often preached, gain nothing by it except the facility of treating with cold indifference both the gracious promises, and the terrible warnings of the Almighty. In the afternoon, Sunday-school was held, for the first time, in the new room, but, before the services could begin, at least ten minutes had to be devoted to the children's exclamations of delight concerning "Such a splendid, beautiful place!" The parents, with a not inexcusable pride and self-gratulation, exchanged remarks to the same effect. Years ago, Hugh had received from Marianna his first religious instructions, and he was now enabled,—though in a very small degree,—to make some repayment, by telling her how things were managed in the city Sunday-schools, as regarded many little details of which she had hitherto been ignorant.

On the following day, Hugh said to Marianna, "Now that my first duty here is accomplished, I will, for awhile, give my whole mind to an effort to do something for Lieutenant Ferrand. First, I must go to Brazil, and learn if he is still alive, and if so, upon what grounds he is kept a prisoner. Then, I will return to New-York, and see if he has no friends or relations who will interest themselves in his behalf."

25*

Marianna warmly approved of this design, and, on the same evening, Hugh explained it before a meeting of the wreckers. Each of the men whom we have mentioned as owning vessels, immediately offered Hugh his services, and the use of his craft, to go to Brazil, and afterwards to New York, for the purpose of making an attempt to liberate Lieutenant Ferrand. Hugh could accept the offer of only one of these men, and, after making a selection, the next day was fixed for the time of starting upon the voyage.

Just before he sailed, Hugh went to take leave of Marianna and Bessie, and to receive their assurance that not a day or night, and, indeed, not one hour of waking life should pass, in which their prayers would not ascend to Heaven for the success of his mission.

"I think," said Marianna, "that, while you are away, you will need more money than

you now have. Take these, and sell them."
As she spoke, she placed in his hand a little
box, containing a pair of diamond ear-drops,
and then went on to say, " Years ago, grandfather got these from some lady who was
drowned upon our coast. He gave them to
me, and now, for the first time, I feel
glad of having them, because they may help
you in trying to restore Bessie's father to
freedom!"

When Hugh bade good-bye to Bessie, and
stooped down to kiss her, she flung her arms
around his neck, and exclaimed, " I will love
you always, if you bring my Papa back to
me again!"

Marianna did not speak, but her swimming
eyes and quivering lip told how deep were
her feelings. The vessel was ready, the wind
was favorable,—and Hugh set sail upon his
voyage.

About a week after this, a large vessel struck, and partially went to pieces, upon a reef opposite the wreckers' settlement. This vessel was very handsomely fitted up, and furnished, and had on board a well assorted cargo,—so that a temptation was here offered to the wreckers, to resume their old habits of greedy and lawless plunder. But there were several men who had openly come out upon the Lord's side, in a little prayer-meeting which, for the last two Sabbath evenings Giles had held in the new Sunday-school room;—and these men had an influence in the community that controlled some others who would willingly have yielded to temptation. Under the direction of Giles and his fellow Christians, every individual on board of the vessel was brought safely to land, before any attempt was made to save the cargo. Among the persons rescued was the owner of the vessel, a wealthy merchant named Le Blanc,—with his wife and three children. Mr. Le Blanc had with him a very large sum of money, in a tin box, but anxiety for the safety of his wife and children caused him to forget this box, and it was left on board of the wreck, where it was found by two of the converted wreckers. They immediately brought it to Le Blanc, saying, " Here, sir, is your money." Surprised and pleased by the honesty and humanity of those among whom he had been thrown, Le Blanc determined that these men should be rewarded in a generous manner. He made a handsome present of money to the two whom we have just mentioned, and to each of those who had been instrumental in saving the lives of himself and family, and he likewise declared that all the wreckers were welcome to divide among themselves the cargo, provisions, and all the vessel's furniture which had been preserved.

"Now," said Giles, to some persons who had murmured and sneered at the plans of reform, "you have said that honesty would be a losing business, but you see that it is not so!"

Mrs. Le Blanc was a Roman Catholic lady, but, like everyone else, she was charmed with Marianna, and was very anxious that she should pay a visit to the city of St. Augustine, where the Le Blancs resided. This was Marianna's first opportunity of visiting a city, and yet she unhesitatingly declined to leave, even for a short time, her grandfather, Bessie and the Sunday-school.

At length, Mr. Le Blanc said, " Well, Miss Von Uldon, if you will come with us for a week or ten days, I will send back with you a nice little library of books for your Sunday-school."

Marianna yielded to this offer, and accompanied the Le Blanc family to St. Augustine. Her going away, even for a short time, caused a deep sensation in the wrecker settlement. Though the people there had always loved and honored Marianna, this first period of her absence from them revealed to their hearts, more plainly than ever before, how very dear and precious this young girl was to all around her. Many of the children and young people viewed her departure with positive alarm and consternation, as though they feared that, when she was absent, all the social and religious frame of things would become disjointed and fall to pieces. Marianna's grandfather was left to the companionship of little Bessie, to whom he had become much attached. While her father was there, and frequently visited the island, to see his child, Von Ulden had not deigned to take any notice of Bessie, lest she should tell Lieutenant Ferrand of his conde-scension. But, since her father was gone, the old man unbent so far as to show that he considered Bessie a pleasant and amusing companion for his otherwise dull and tedious hours. She gained upon his favor more rapidly by her frank and fearless disposition, which caused her to talk to Von Ulden as freely as to any one else, and, when he said things which were meant to tease and dis-concert her, she often answered him with a saucy archness at which the old man would grimly smile.

As we have said, St. Augustine was the first city Marianna had ever visited, and on arriving there, she saw around her as much that was new and wonderful as most people would notice at Constantinople, or Cairo.

"Ah!" said Mrs. Le Blanc, "just wait until Sunday, and go with me to church, and you will see the finest sight of all!"

When Marianna entered the Catholic Church which Mrs. Le Blanc attended, she became dizzy with astonishment and admiration. The architecture, the paintings, the rich adornments, and the music, were unlike any thing she had ever thought or dreamed of before. Yet, when the Catholic lady proudly inquired if this was not the best church to go to, Marianna innocently replied, "Oh, Mrs. Le Blanc, it is very splendid, but it does not feel like a church!"

Mr. Le Blanc kept his promise, and provided Marianna with a nice little Sunday-school library to take home with her. All the elder children had, by this time, learned to

26

read, and, when this treasure of books arrived, they thought themselves the most
favored persons upon earth. The next Sabbath after her return, on entering the Sunday-school room, she was received with
cheering demonstrations of welcome. When
she had an opportunity of speaking quietly
aside with Mrs. Giles, she remarked, "How
much more pleasant this place is, than the
grand Catholic church where I went with
Mrs. Le Blanc! The painted glass windows
looked very rich, but they kept out the light,
so that one could scarcely tell whether it
was night or day; and, they have great tall
candles burning all the time, in that huge
gloomy church, like glow-worms in a cave!
Now, here, we have God's own light; and
the sunshine, streaming in so cheerfully upon the pure white walls, makes me think of
the brightness that is in one's heart, when

the gospel truth has lighted it up, and the Holy Spirit has purified it! Instead of burning incense, filling the place with its smoke and sickly smell, we have the scent of fresh flowers, coming in at the open windows. Instead of singing in a strange language, that one cannot tell a word of,—we have those dear hymns, that seem as if they were telling in music the innermost thoughts of our hearts;—and even the sound of the great organ is not so grand and solemn as that roaring of the sea that comes from the beach!"

CHAPTER XIII.

EVER since Marianna first commenced her Sunday-school, Bessie had repeatedly asked " Grandfather," as she called Von Ulden, to go there with her and he had always refused. Marianna and Mrs. Giles, had given the same invitation, but in vain. One Sabbath, Bessie was particularly importunate, and, partly to humor her, and partly to pass away the time, Von Ulden consented to go. It was the first time that he had been over to the main land since that occasion, years ago, when the scorn and

26*

insolence of the wreckers had driven him to return, in an agony of rage and mortification, to his lonely island.

But now, when the aged man entered the Sunday-school room with one hand grasping his staff, and the other held by little Bessie, every one gazed at him in silence, and with a deeper seriousness than usual. Marianna hastened to provide him with a comfortable seat, and Giles, coming up, shook hands with him, and expressed his satisfaction at seeing him there. Von Ulden sat in silence, with his eyes fixed upon the floor, and features as grim and rigid as usual.

When the children joined their voices in singing a hymn, Von Ulden suddenly raised his eyes and looked around at them. Now, the Sunday-school boys and girls of the wrecker settlement were all clean and neat in their dress, and the appearance of both

scholars and parents betokened a decent
pride that had once been unknown to them.
Many of the children were pretty and interesting.   Their faces showed their earnest interest in the hymn that flowed so sweetly
from their lips.   No human heart is all of
stone, and Von Ulden never was so easily
softened as in the presence of childhood ;—
for men and women had given him only
what he imagined were just causes to hate
them.   It had been many, many years since
he had heard such music as the artless melody
of those childish voices, and there seemed to
thrill within his breast a chord which had
been so long untouched that he had forgotten
its existence.   Again he cast down his eyes,
but now all his features seemed to be working with the effect to surpress a deep, un-
wonted emotion.

It seemed, however, that it was not an un-

pleasant one, for, on each succeeding Sabbath
Von Ulden suffered himself to be led by little Bessie to that hallowed place. His chief
object was to listen to the singing of the
children, and it was marvellous to see a soft-
ening and humanizing tear sometimes glide
down the deeply furrowed cheek of the aged
and hardened man!

One Sabbath evening, Marianna invited
her grandfather to go with her to the prayer-
meeting, and he consented. Several persons
arose in succession, to tell what the Lord had
done for them, or to ask the prayers of others
in their behalf. As the meeting was about
to conclude, Von Ulden half arose, but seemed
to change his mind, and was about to sink
back again, when Marianna placed her hand
beneath his arm, and whispering, " Yes, dear
grandfather,"—gently assisted him to his
feet. There was silence for a moment or

two, and then, in hoarse and faltering tones, Von Ulden said, "I was going to ask you to pray for me,—but it is of no use;—I am too wicked. There is no hope for such a man as I am!"

"Yes, there is!" cried Giles, "The lamp of life is still burning!—Jesus still says, 'Come!'"—And he and two others poured out supplications of heart-warm fervor, that light from Heaven might dawn upon Von Ulden's soul. The old man was greatly moved, yet, he was not able to realize that there could be mercy for him. But,—"Oh, the height and depth of the goodness of God!"—After a severe spiritual struggle of several days and nights, Von Ulden found peace at the foot of the Cross. He never said much concerning his feelings, but, all could see, by his words, and ways, and actions, that he had become a new creature.

Marianna received a letter from Hugh, conveying deeply interesting tidings from Brazil. He had learned that Lieutenant Ferrand was still alive, and imprisoned in a certain fortress, but he was not permitted to see him. However, Hugh had held a long conversation with the American Consul at Rio, and by relating Lieutenant Ferrand's whole history, had so far interested our Consul that he immediately applied to the Brazilian authorities, upon the prisoner's behalf. The authorities agreed, as a compromise, to release Ferrand, if a large sum of money was paid down, by way of fine; and Hugh was now about to start for New York, in order to see if such an amount could be raised by applying to the Lieutenant's friends.

Six weeks more elapsed, when, one bright lovely morning, there was seen coming over the sunny ocean, a vessel which was quickly

recognized as the craft that had carried Hugh
from Florida. Those who first saw it hastened to communicate the news to others, and
every man, woman or child, in the settlement
who was able to leave his or her dwelling,
came hurrying down to the beach. Marianna and Bessie ran to the island shore, and
stood gazing speechlessly at the coming vessel, each with her hands clasped tightly together.

At some distance from the shore, the vessel cast anchor, and a small boat was lowered,
into which four men descended. The little
boat rowed quickly toward's Von Ulden's
island, and, soon, all who were gazing towards it saw that two of the men were
wreckers, who held the oars, another was
Hugh, and the fourth was Lieutenant Ferrand.

Loud cheers, and shouts of joy, burst from

all the groups who were gathered upon the snowy beach, and the wreckers in the boat shouted in return ; but Lieutenant Ferrand and Hugh could only take off their hats and wave them to the crowd, in silence.

"Minna, isn't that my Papa, sitting by Hugh?" fairly shrieked Bessie.

"It is !"—gasped the almost fainting Marianna.

The boat, as we have said, was rowed towards Von Ulden's island, and, presently, Lieutenant Ferrand sprang upon the shore. Bessie flew to meet him, and when he lifted her in his arms, she clung about his neck as though determined, by holding him thus, to prevent the risk of ever being separated from her father again. Marianna sank down upon her knees on the sand ;—it was the only position that seemed natural to her at such a moment. Her cheeks were pale, yet her face was radiant;—her hands were folded over her bosom, and her eyes raised to Heaven in an ecstacy of gratitude and devotion. Hugh stood by in silence, but he would not have exchanged the feelings of that never-to-be-forgotten moment for a whole life-time of selfish pleasure. It was such a moment as seems to atone for years of darkness and trouble, and to vindicate the goodness of Providence in mysteries we cannot fathom.

Hugh had obtained a part of the large sum required for Ferrand's release from the Lieutenant's wealthy relatives; but the greater portion was contributed by old friends, who had not forgotten how they had been benefitted by Ferrand's generosity, in the days when he was rich and prosperous. We will not attempt to describe the emotions felt upon both sides, when Hugh appeared in Ferrand's prison, to tell him that his captiv-

27

ity was at an end. The poor boy, upon whose account he had incurred his suspension from the navy, was revealed as the liberator and benefactor of him for whose kindness it had once seemed impossible that he should ever make the least return!

Ferrand had raised Marianna from her kneeling attitude upon the sand, and was holding her hands clasped in his, when the sound of tottering steps was heard, and Von Ulden appeared, leaning upon his staff. He extended his hand to the returned prisoner, and said, "Come to my house, Lieutenant Ferrand. It was once a tiger's den;—it is now the dwelling of a poor, repentant sinner!"

"Yes, dear sir," said Hugh, "do go to Mr. Von Ulden's house, and I will cross over to the mainland, and tell the people that you will receive their congratulations to-morrow.

Lieutenant Ferrand was not nearly so

much broken down by his long confinement
as Marianna and Hugh had apprehended he
would be, and, during the trip from Brazil,
he had regained not a little of the strength
which he had lost,—yet the effects of his imprisonment were easily to be seen. Close
confinement, and prison fare, had blanched
the clear light brownish tint of his complexion to a chalky white, and he was thinner
than he had ever been before. Something
of nervousness appeared in his manner, especially in the wild brightness of his eyes,
as he darted them around at those beautiful
and familiar scenes from which, but lately, he
had seemed to be cut off forever. Yet, he
acted and spoke with surprising energy and
cheerfulness, considering the severe ordeal
through which he had passed, and his sudden
change of situation.

Lieutenant Ferrand had been seated in

Von Ulden's house but a few moments, when Giles and his wife called to see him. Hugh had informed the wreckers that the Lieutenant's present strength was not equal to any more excitement that day, but that he would see them the next morning. Giles, however, could not.wait even this long before he gave utterance to what was weighing upon his mind. On entering Lieutenant Ferrand's presence, Giles was greatly agitated, but he did not offer to approach and shake hands, until the Lientenant came up to him, and taking his hand, said, "Well, my old friend Giles, I am sure that you are glad to see me!"

"Oh, my dear, injured friend," sobbed the old sailor, "I am glad to have the chance, that I have so often longed for, of asking your forgiveness;—and yet I am cut to the heart to think that my selfish persuasions,—

and my arguments that were meant to deceive both myself and you,—led you to be a wrecker, and caused this sad misfortune!"

"Never mind," said Lieutenant Ferrand, gently and kindly, " we both know better now than we did then. I suppose the misfortune you allude to is my being shut up in prison;—but, in one respect, it has proved a great blessing to me."

"How is that?" said Marianna; "Please tell us the whole history, Lieutenant."

The Lieutenant complied with her request, but we will tell the story somewhat more briefly than he did. When Ferrand first realized that he was a prisoner for a long time,—perhaps for life, the idea was so insupportable that he threw himself against the iron-bound door of his cell, as a wild bird, when newly caged, will sometimes dash itself against the wires of its prison. Then,

27*

exhausted in mind and body, he sank upon his coarse, hard bed, and lay for hours in a trance-like state, while confused and changing images of his past life like a moving panorama swept before him.   His jailers fully expected that he would soon either die or go mad, and, on a certain day, one of them said to him, "Well, American, you may be a fine blade at fighting, but I never saw such a poor hand at standing this cage!"

Ferrand experienced a feeling of shame at this, and determined that, in future, he would display more fortitude.   He knew that, in order to do so, he must have some way of occupying his mind, and he thought of various devices which he had read of as being employed by other unhappy prisoners, to while away their time,—but none of them seemed practicable there.   What would he not have given for a book!   But then the thought struck him that he had a book,—the little Bible that Blanche had given him upon her dying bed, and which the prison authorities had permitted him to retain. Blanche had told him, too, that in that book he would find comfort for life's darkest hour; and he knew that it would furnish him with at least some occupation for his mind. The study of this precious volume now became his daily employment. After reading the whole Bible attentively through, he resolved to commit a large portion of it to memory, and, during his imprisonment, he learned the whole of the New Testament, besides the Psalms, and other parts of the Old. As we have intimated, Ferrand undertook this merely to give employment to his mind, but the result was far greater than he had expected. Can any one commit to memory, and study over, the recorded words of Jesus, and yet fail to find them melt his heart and penetrate his soul? Often, as Ferrand repeated some precept, his conscience told him that he had willfully transgressed it, and he felt that had he taken the Bible for his guide, he would never have been shut up in a prison cell, as the leader of a band of wicked and lawless men. He who had always before been ashamed to own, even before God, that he was a great sinner, now bowed his head in shame and self reproach at the thought of his own folly in cherishing such a fatal pride of heart. Yet, deeply convinced as he was of his life-long error,—he did not despair; for those who study the Bible as attentively as Ferrand did, cannot fail to learn the true remedy for sin. He acknowledged his utter helplessness, and threw himself entirely upon the merits of Christ. He knelt upon the stone floor of his cell in daily prayer, and enjoyed long and sweet seasons of communion with the Saviour. He fancied that the spirits of his sainted wife and mother were bending over him with approval and joy, and he now felt sure that death, even should it come to him in a prison, would restore their society to him forever.

While repeating some favorite passages from the Bible, Ferrand would walk up and down the room, for exercise, which did much to preserve his bodily health. His Bible was the talisman that enabled him to pass through his imprisonment without losing life or reason, and with a resignation which no human philosophy could possibly have supplied.

Marianna was delighted, but not surprised, by hearing of Ferrand's conversion, for, she had always felt in her heart that so many prayers of true faith could not be lost upon

the ear of Infinite Love and Mercy. Her
face was radiant, while, as hostess, she received the successive parties of wreckers
who came to offer their congratulations to
Lieutenant Ferrand, within the once shun-
ned and forbidden precints of Von Ulden's
island !

The next day was Sunday, and the Lieutenant went with his little girl, and Marianna,
and her grandfather, to attend the religious
services upon the main land. As they were
coming to Florida, Hugh had told him of
those wonderful changes which had taken
place among the wreckers, yet, as he walked
through the village, he looked around with
continued astonishment, When he thought
of the wrecker settlement as he had last seen
it,—it seemed as though this truly Sabbath-
like stillness, and all these neatly dressed
families going to the house of worship,—must

be features of some strange and pleasant dream.

"After all," said Ferrand to Marianna, with a smile that was full of feeling, "you were to be the great reformer!"

"No,—no,"—said Marianna, hastily, "it was not I;—it was the religion of Jesus!"

Hugh preached again, that morning, and we need scarcely say that to see Hugh in the sacred desk, and to hear him deliver an excellent discourse, was another subject of grateful meditation for Lieutenant Ferrand. That afternoon, Ferrand was present at the session of the Sunday-school, and as he gazed upon those who were there assembled, he saw many whose faces had been familiar to him two years before, but who had now undergone a wondrous transformation. Among these was the girl who had been called by the title of "Spunkey Poll," and who, until

Mrs. Ferrand bribed her by the gift of a much handsomer article of the same kind, had been so unwilling to give up the gold chain taken from the drowned body of Mrs. Stillingwell's son. Polly was in the class which Marianna taught, and she was most fondly attached to her young teacher. There was not a girl in the whole school of neater personal appearance, or more modest and quiet in her behaviour. She now utterly disclaimed her old nickname, and gave good evidence of being deeply impressed upon the subject of religion, so that Marianna hoped soon to see her stand forth as a pro-professed disciple of the Saviour.

Von Ulden sat near little Bessie, and directly by the side of her father,—his hands resting upon the top of his staff, and his hoary head bent in reverent attention, as, after a long life of sin and profanity, he, at

last, received the truths of the Gospel with
the meekness of a little child. Lieutenant
Ferrand wore an expression so full of be-
nignity and happiness that, even to those who
had always looked upon him with admiring
eyes, his countenance now seemed almost
transfigured. And what a cheering scene
was this to Marianna! But we will not attempt to describe the perfect joy that filled
her heart. Let those who would understand
it, go and taste for themselves the delight of
being God's instruments in bringing immortal souls from death unto life!

After the close of the regular exercises,
Ferrand rose and addressed the children in
some affectionate and encouraging remarks,
which were listened to with intense interest.
At the evening prayer-meeting, he, for the
first time, prayed aloud in public, and then,
in a modest and touching manner, related his

28
.

religious experience, while a prisoner in Brazil.

About two weeks afterwards, Von Ulden was attacked by an illness which, though slight at first, soon proved too severe for so aged and feeble a frame. It was an early afternoon in early summer, when Marianna, Mr. and Mrs. Giles, Lieutenant Ferrand, and Hugh, assembled around the dying bed of Von Ulden. The sunbeams, stealing through the flowering vines that overhung an open window, scattered spots of brightness over the snowy counterpane and pillows, and the no less snowy hair and beard of the now departing wrecker.

"If it had not been for Divine grace," said he to Marianna, " this hour would have separated you and me forever ;—but, we know that it is not for long.—Young man," he added, addressing Hugh, " when you

28

preach, you must often tell the people that the blood of Christ saved even old Von Ulden.

After a moment's silence, the old man added, " Lieutenant Ferrand, I should like to hear you pray."

All knelt down, while Ferrand, though, at first, his voice trembled, from a feeling of deep solemnity of this scene, prayed aloud, with the inspired earnestness of a glowing Christian faith, and Christian love. When they arose, Von Ulden's eyes were tranquilly closed, and his hands lay, lightly folded before him. He had fallen asleep in Jesus.

All the people in the wrecker settlement attended as mourners the funeral of "the old Commodore," whom they had once treated with unfeeling contempt, and who had repaid them with savage hatred, before the Holy Spirit had performed the greatest of all miracles,—that of creating anew his heart. Every one looked with an increased respect and tenderness upon the now orphaned Marianna, yet they felt that she was not, and never would be left really alone.

Soon after Von Ulden's death, Lieutenant Ferrand was restored to that position in the Navy from which he had been temporarily suspended;—but whether on the ocean or the land, his Christian graces always shone so brightly as to make him a " living epistle, known and read of all men."

Marianna had trained and guarded Bessie with such zealous care, during her father's imprisonment, that Lieutenant Ferrand resolved still to leave his child under the same charge, and he provided every facility for Bessie's receiving a first-class education, without being removed from the faithful and loving eyes of Marianna.

Hugh Ross left to finish his theological studies, but he bore with him an earnest call from the people of his native village, that a minister might come to dispense to them regularly the word of life, from the desk of their beloved Sunday-school room. Their wish was granted. A prosperous church now gathers in its still increasing throng of worshippers, from that region where all was ignorance, lawlessness, and spiritual darkness, until the first Sabbath-school was there commenced by the wrecker's grand-child.

We have seen that through the instrumentality of Marianna, great changes were wrought in the community where she lived. Yet, she had not displayed any very extraordinary gifts of intellect. Her power

28*

lay in an unwavering faith in God, an ardent love for the souls of others, and in that energy and perseverance which sincere faith and love naturally inspire. She had not aimed to do any great or marvellous thing. All that she did was quietly, earnestly, and thoroughly, to improve every opportunity of honoring Jesus, and of turning the attention of others, not to herself, but to Him who is "able to save even to the uttermost."

THE END.

www.ingramcontent.com/pod-product-compliance
Lightning Source LLC
Chambersburg PA
CBHW020939030726
47496CB00005B/1270